Twisted Intentions

by

Seven Rodgers

Cover Art by *Tina Lynn Stout*

The Wild Rose Press, Inc.
PO Box 708
Adams Basin, NY 14410-0708
Visit us at www.thewildrosepress.com

Publishing History
First Edition, 2025
Trade Paperback ISBN
Digital ISBN

Previously Published 2021
Published in the United States of America

Dedication

For my son, Luke.
My miracle, my hero.

Chapter 1

Charlotte

Eighteen years old! Finally, I'm an adult and can escape this single-wide that reeks of spilled liquor, cigarettes, and pot. My older sister, Blair, will assist with that; she's moving me into her condo today. Maybe I can find some normalcy and figure out a direction in life there, but Blair must first push through our mother, Regena.

Regena warned me enough times to take her seriously. "You'll leave this home over my dead body."

I argued in my usual non-combative tone. "It's not a home. It's a noisy, dilapidated tin can squatting beside a busy highway that blows dirt and sand into the windows. We're stuck with fifteen other crumbling trailers squeezed onto an acre covered in weeds that climb over abandoned cars, bicycles, and engine parts. It's a hell hole."

Holding on to a chair helps my mother from swaying like a drunken sailor. "Pfft … such a high and mighty freak. I do the best I can. Others have it worse."

Blair decided to rescue me from Regena last week. She couldn't even eyeball the ragged person Mother had become—toothless mouth and craggy facial creases that sag lopsidedly from a meth-induced stroke. My sister, a blonde Barbie doll, focused on the floor while she spoke

1

forcefully, shuffling backward toward the only exit.

"Charlotte turns eighteen next week and will be a legal adult; I'm moving her in with me, and there's nothing you can do about it. I'll be here in a week, Little Sis, so pack your things."

Bang! Blair let the front door slam behind her.

"Sure, you run away. I'm not so fast as you anymore… damn arthritis," Regena screamed as she hobbled across the room. Throwing open the screen door, her straw hair whipping her face in the breeze, she stuck out her middle finger, spitting poison as Blair's BMW peeled down the street.

"You ungrateful wretch. If it weren't for me, you'd be cashiering in some greasy spoon. Go to hell and take your thankless freak-sister with you. Leave me here alone…"

After the fight, Regena's usual drama swelled out of proportion. "Both my girls are abandoning me. Y'all are ashamed of me," she whines, hanging her head. Then, like someone pushed a rage button, she switches gears. "Well, fuck you. It's your fault men won't stay with me. They know you're a freak. But you go on. Step outside this house; you'll find out."

Mother took a break from her haranguing and, after more vodka, saw an even bleaker life ahead.

"It don't matter if you are here or not. Nobody wants me anymore. I'm too old for 'em. I'm ancient with a freak smart-ass daughter—talks like she knows everything when she bothers talking—like some fucking computer with legs."

Mother dearest ceased eating, washed down more booze, and turned silent as a statue—not one bitchy, vomit-us word escaped from her painted lips. Perfect timing, too, because I am officially an adult with choices. Regena's drama will not mar my day.

I slip off my paper-thin mattress, stretch, and then head to the bathroom when I hear a chair scraping across the kitchen floor. I drag myself there to see Regena's silly smile as she holds a gun … to her head. BANG!

Brains land on me as they fly to the wall, where they spatter. Regena crumples onto the linoleum at my feet, blood oozing down the uneven floor like a slow, winding creek.

No screams. No horror. No surprise. Her dramatic exit doesn't faze me. Mother has freed me after all.

I dial nine-one-one and only give them our address. In our section of town, the police take their time. While waiting for the god-awful crowd that will gather soon, I shower off grey matter that drips from my hair. I wash my spattered pj's and hang them to dry out back. I catch myself humming. Honestly, her death begins my birth. For the first time in my life, peace flows through me. Happy Birthday to me.

Now, I call Blair.

"Oh, God, no! This isn't your fault; I pushed her too hard. I'm on my way there—wait outside. Tell the police to call me. Oh, God."

Although capable of handling the situation, I follow Blair's orders like a compliant little sister. She arrives, confessing hysterically to the police that she should have known Regena would commit suicide.

"She was an alcoholic, pill popper, and used every drug under the sun. She's been getting meaner. She lost it even more when I told her I was moving Charlotte in with me. Oh God, I shouldn't have pushed her. Little Sis was all she had."

After the police conclude their reports on the "obvious" suicide of a low-life, I move in with Blair, quickly leaving Mother's death behind. But, Blair wants to discuss it. "She was too self-centered for suicide, and she was such a klutz. That gun sat on top of the fridge for months. When did she learn to use it?"

Other thoughts pop into her head, too. "What would make her get up early in the morning anyway? She used to sleep until noon."

"I doubt she went to bed at all that night."

I must devise a way to take my grieving sister's mind off our miserable excuse for a mother.

****

Charlotte - Six months later

Blair obsesses over me and prods me with questions like, "Are you happy?" Usually, I lie when asked about emotions. 'Sure' and 'Of course' are my standard replies, but they don't convince my worried sister, who is too concerned, too preoccupied with my state of mind after our irrational childhoods close like a Broadway tragedy from Regena's suicide.

I try reassuring her. "I am fortunate, especially for a college student, Blair. Instead of coping with a noisy dorm room or living with a throng of potheads in a downtown rental, I live with you a world away from the trailer park."

Her condominium is on picturesque Amelia Island, the most Northeastern island in Florida. My view overlooks blush-colored pampas surrounding a natural pond visited by wild geese. I breathe in the salty ocean breeze that mixes with the sweet smell of freshly mowed St. Augustine grass. Natural settings soothe me, so I'm not yanking her leg to appease her. I am sincerely grateful.

Unlike my previous neighbors, her cheerful residents drive Mercedes, BMWs, and modern SUVs. They even invest in designer décor for their decks and balconies. But our patio, with its miserable staging of two Wal-Mart chairs and a small PVC side table, begs for classier tastes—even the plastic hummingbird feeder swings empty in the breeze.

Since Blair insists we hide our trailer-trash beginnings, I suggest that she carry the same design principle she uses inside the condo to the balcony. But she cares nothing about my décor ideas. She is consumed with me and my 'withdrawn behavior.' I don't know why; I show her every respect because she merits it.

Although her dating life trails that of other women her age, Blair scales the corporate ladder, using her astonishing math skills as an actuary and earning a healthy income. But instead of focusing on a social life, she fills her cloistered time with another project; unfortunately, that mission is me.

When the front door opens, professional Blair morphs into a big sister, talking about feelings and overstepping my emotional boundaries. Not this evening—I plan to throw her off track and move her in another direction so she will stop throwing impossible questions at me like, "Are you happy?"

"Charlotte, I'm home. How were your classes today?" Blair follows routine as she breezes into the condo.

I enjoy another breath of fresh air before stepping inside to make the first move.

"Blair, what happened to those college friends of yours?" I'm confident she will swallow the girlfriend bait, hooked by curiosity like a cat chasing a mouse.

"My college friends? You mean Debbie, Meghan, and Samantha?" Blair flips through the mail in her usual unstylish three-piece office attire: a skirt, blouse, and jacket, no matter the season—always navy, tan, or gray with matching plain pumps.

"Well, after they graduated from Jacksonville University, Sam and Debbie began careers in this area while Meghan entered law school." Blair sets down the mail and leans against the granite-top breakfast bar as I count the seconds before she answers. "You know, Little Sis, I don't understand why we drifted apart; we were besties. Except for yearly Christmas cards, we lost touch."

"That's odd, isn't it, considering how close y'all were?" I prod until the proverbial light bulb goes off in her head.

"For heaven's sake, yes; they all live nearby. It isn't as though everyone moved to other areas. I don't know why we're estranged except for beginning careers that monopolized days and nights. Why do you ask?"

"Oh, they crossed my mind when I saw your bird feeder."

Blair smiles. "Oh, yes, we were quite the animal advocates in college. We began the campus rescue—everything from cats and dogs to birds with broken wings. I hear it's still operating." She stares down at her feet for a few seconds and sighs. "We made a united team with big plans to continue good works after graduation—but like I said, careers and all." She pulls out a barstool and sits.

"Still, I've adapted to job demands; I bet they have too. Jacksonville may be the largest city in Florida, but it's not so big that it should separate four friends. With all the new highways to Amelia, we live only minutes apart now."

I don't argue.

"You know, Little Sis, I'm going to resolve this situation." She picks up what she calls "the new contraption," a smartphone. "What's the name of that search engine you go on about?"

"It's been around for a few years; it's called Google. You might want to try Facebook, too. Um, aren't you supposed to be the geek in the family?"

"Ha! I've fallen behind in everything. The company still treats me like a fledgling; they overload me with work. But I'm finished with their games; no more bringing home tasks." She kicks her briefcase aside. "It's time I start enjoying a social life; I miss my friends."

Bingo. Blair-kitty catches the mouse. I've already checked; the search for her friends will be successful. If my plan works, my big sister will stop draining the life out of me by probing my psyche, seeking forgiveness for coming too late to my rescue, and shouldering responsibility for our years apart.

Re-introducing her to long-lost best friends is a stroke of genius. Freedom will ring for me when she locates them and arranges a get-together. A knock on my bedroom door pulls me back to earth.

"What's up, Blair?"

"You must come to our reunion, Little Sis. After all, you gave me the push I needed to reach out to the girls. They are expecting you."

I hate it when she raises that eyebrow. Has my scheme failed?

"You are becoming a recluse. I'm afraid you'll end

up like Regena… alone, alcohol and drug-addicted, blowing your brains out with a semi-automatic."

Not likely. I'm not a weakling. Maybe Blair needs me along for show like a rescued pet? I'll play the part a while longer until I'm not needed to fill her void. Maybe there is still hope for my plan!

If not, I'll head out on my own.

Chapter 2

Blair and I arrive early at Sandy Bottoms, an ocean-front bar and grill on Amelia Island. It was the old college hangout for her and her friends, perfect for a reunion. Tourists pack the high-ceiling, brick-walled room. Luckily, we find a two-top and hope for a larger table soon.

"Oh dear, I forgot about Memorial Day weekend." Blair never remembers or celebrates holidays. "If you see any extra chairs, grab them, Little Sis. Let's hope we can scoop up a few before the other gals arrive."

Suddenly, a familiar face sneaks up behind Blair. The woman places an index finger on her lips so I don't spoil the surprise. She puts her hands over Blair's eyes.

"Oh, my." My startled sister breathes in deeply.

"I know who this is...Debbie!" Blair pops off the barstool and hugs her friend for a long minute. Breaking free, they stand inches apart and study each other's faces.

Debbie places her hands on her hips. "How ever did you know it was me?"

"Bal A Versailles. You know I love that perfume."

"I remember, so enjoy it tonight. I'm wearing the last of the original formula from the seventies —a gift from my mother. They stopped production, and the fakes don't compare. I've been trying other brands; Petit Mort is heavenly."

Blair's cheeks redden. "I'm not familiar with it."

9

That perfume costs more than most women make in a month. Unlike Blair, I read everything about current culture.

Born into generational wealth and society, Debbie Williams breathes a life of privilege, looking the part, too, but with a professor's edge., Her blonde hair, pulled straight back and up, shows off beautiful diamond stud earrings. I'm assuming it's Tiffany. They match the diamond bracelet and what appears to be a white-gold necklace with the same size diamond as her earrings.

"Debbie's designer clothes are resort casual — Bermuda shorts and silk top; but she wears Italian platform sandals, so she stands inches taller than Blair's five-foot-three. Without a word, her manner says classy and influential.

"Hey, you started the love fest without me? Move over!"

We hear her sharp, trill voice before we see her. Samantha crams between Blair and Debbie, giving each friend a fierce four-foot-ten hug. Her black-spiked pixie adds a half-inch to her height. Samantha Yu, most always called Sam, is their exotic friend who entered the United States from Taiwan at age eighteen. Blair says she is a tough cookie. I agree, sensing Sam's underlying street smarts and recognizing that she is different, maybe even 'freakish' like my dearly departed mother called me.

"God, Sam, it's so good to see you." Blair towers over her tiny frame.

"Really? All this time, and no one calls? I thought you forget about me."

I sense that Sam is only half-joking.

"Samantha, no one could ever forget the wonder

nerd!" Meghan steps through the crowd.

"Aiya! Megs!" Sam hugs Meghan, who is in flat loafers and stands at least two inches taller than Debbie.

Meghan laughs at Sam's antics and finally gets her share of hugs from each friend.

Blair said that Meghan Kent grew up middle-class with a strict, church-going, law-abiding, stay-at-home mom and an accountant father who ruled with an iron will. She never drank until she met Sam and then Blair and Debbie. She was rigid in her mindset, too, until she got involved with the girls. She still looks too prim and proper to me, the kind with a two-by-four up her ass. Meghan's hair is auburn, and she is fiercely bony with no fat. Her pretty, cherub-like face sprinkled with freckles gives her a girl-next-door appearance with model potential.

The four friends stand there, giggling like young schoolgirls. Suddenly, Debbie announces, "On three." She stretches her hand to the center of their circle, saying, "I can."

Blair places her hand on top. "I can."

Meghan does the same. "I can."

Sam tiptoes to reach the top. "I can."

Four professionals, hands in place, turn in a full circle together. Then they holler: "We can change the world." Every head in Sandy Bottoms turns to see what the shouting is about. The ladies are giggling and hugging again. When will they resume their professional personas and stop acting so puerile?

Blair points to me. "You remember Little Sis, don't you?" She hurries off to scavenge more chairs.

"Little? You aren't little anymore. How tall are you?" Sam gazes up at me admiringly.

"Six feet."

"You must be out of high school by now, right?" Meghan asks sharply, like I'm on trial.

"Yes, ma'am. I'm finishing my freshman year at State."

Meghan continues to pry. "Have you decided on a major?"

"No, I'm undecided."

"Little Sis, you've grown into a beauty with that gorgeous black hair."

"Thank you, Miss Debbie."

"Miss Debbie? I'm not that old, darlin.' Call me Debbie and drop the ma'am, too. I understand Southern protocols better than most, but you are our Little Sis. No need for formalities here."

That's nice. I appreciate the respect.

Blair pulls up two chairs. "Oh, there, one more behind you, Little Sis." Dutifully, I set the chair next to me, and Sam quickly selects it as a pressured server arrives.

"I'm sorry, ladies. We're shorthanded and didn't expect such a crowd until tomorrow. What can I get y'all?"

"Bottle of wine for old time's sake?" Blair asks her friends.

"Sure. Bring the best Pinot Noir and put it on my tab under Debbie. And you better keep the bottles coming, sweetie. Oh, and for Little Sis?"

"Cranberry juice."

"Certainly. Would you like any food tonight?" I suspect our server is thrilled at the prospect of a good tip.

"Maybe later, but we'd like to visit first," Debbie speaks for everyone.

"Okay. I'll bring the wine right away." The young server hurries to the manager, who nods his head. He leaves for a few minutes and returns with a bottle that Debbie inspects, tastes, and approves. As I expected, four grown women begin to gossip about the old days. I'm tired of the memory lane talk already.

"Here's some nachos and dip —on the house." The server's lengthy pigtail falls on the table.

Sam's eyes are glued on the cutie, who wears a sea-blue Sandy Bottom's tank that she stretches out to the fullest. The white short shorts show off a figure, too, but apparently, Sam prefers breasts. All the female servers dress the same, but Sam zeroes in on ours.

I thought as much.

"What is your name, sweetie?" Sam's sharp voice changes to smooth honey.

"Jessie. I forgot to introduce myself, didn't I? Sorry."

"It's okay, we know now, Jessie."

"If you need anything at all, please let me know." Her sneakers squeak as she scurries away, winding around the crowd to other tables.

Meghan leans over. "She's not your type."

Sam winks. "I know. It doesn't hurt to notice the topography."

Meghan giggles. "Not topography. Scenery is the more appropriate word."

Sam nods, mouthing the word scenery. According to Blair, she hardly spoke English when she first began college, but Meghan always had her back, teaching and expanding her vocabulary.

Conversation becomes difficult as the bar fills to standing-room-only, and the ladies must speak up to be

13

heard.

Debbie lifts her glass. "Ladies, I suggest a toast. To us! May we never let the years come between us again."

"Never." Each gal clinks her glass, insisting that I toast, too.

Blair asks a question out of the blue. "Speaking of 'never,' do you remember that boy in college who tried reciting Edgar Allen Poe's The Raven?"

"Oh, goodness. That poor boy. Who forgets the *nevermore* line?" Meghan says critically.

"Yeah. The student body ridiculed him like they did me when I tried out for chorus," Samantha pouts. The ladies guffaw at the memory. "Hey, not funny. I love to sing, you know that."

"Yes, and I bet you sound great singing in Chinese," Meghan says, playing the sympathy card.

"I do! I do sound great!" Sam defends herself. "Do they have Karaoke here?"

"No!" Meghan, Blair, and Debbie say in unison.

I look at Blair questioningly; that's a story she never shared with me.

"Ignore them, Little Sis. One day, I sing for you and not just in Chinese."

"Sam, self-deception is a cruel taskmaster. You should have learned your lesson when your try-out video went viral."

Meghan mothers Sam. Hmm, that's an interesting dynamic.

"Aiya." Sam reacts rebelliously, crossing her arms over her chest.

Meghan leans over and gives her a quick hug. "We love you, Sam."

Blair enjoys this reunion, as do her friends. But I

hope the memory lane routine wears off because I can't relate. Besides, I hate boredom and resort to staring out the window. Suddenly, a flock of pelicans flies just above the water towards a dolphin pod that frolics close to shore, probably enjoying the fresh fish that fill our waters.

Before the sun sets, tourists crowd in front of the enormous picture window and block my view. As they empty the second bottle of wine, I'm ready to call a cab to take me home.

But Debbie's tone changes from lightheartedness to something more serious, catching my attention.

Chapter 3

Debbie clinks her glass against Blair's to quiet everyone. I hope she improves the sophomoric reunion with something interesting. Deb commands respect, but having money does that. As she talks, the socialite points her glass at each friend, speaking with the southern lilt of a finely schooled woman.

"… Listen, ladies, and I use that term loosely; we earned degrees and enjoy fulfilling careers, but what happened to our convictions and hope to help the animal world and even change it? We can change the world, remember?

"I'm a professor trying to teach students about our troubled planet. How do I teach this new generation of computer zombies how to affect change when I haven't accomplished any? We were animal advocates. We established our college rescue, but have we done anything since? I saw a puppy hanging by its neck like a piñata from a neighborhood tree just today. Who knows? A sociopath might have killed it for fun or spite."

"Oh, God, that's sick." Blair pales as she mumbles. "Was it dead, or did you save it?"

"Save it? It was dead. Someone hung it and left it there for everyone to see."

"Oh. I was hoping for a happy ending; I can't stand the thought of it."

"Yes, I know what you mean, Blair; girlfriends,

can't you see? We've all become complacent, going through life doing what we do, forgetting the societal changes we wanted to implement for homeless and abused pets since most people are unable or unwilling to get involved.

"We discussed this years ago. Most humans are ostriches, hiding their heads in the sand, hoping to avoid upsetting events because they wouldn't know what to do about it anyway."

Blair shifts on her stool, uncomfortable with the topic. "I understand how they feel. We're four smart cookies crammed around a two-top, allowing years to roll by, forgetting the ideal lives we wanted to live. But you are right; we have become the people we detested in college—normal cogs in the wheel."

Samantha interrupts. "Aiya. Five, Blair, five cookies." Sam nods her head towards me.

Meghan purses her lips and holds up her hand like a shy student might do. "You guys…you live the lives you planned. But I, well, fate won with me. You were right in saying my heart was too mushy. I dropped out of law school."

The reaction is intense silence because everyone knows of Meghan's sharp mind. Blair had bragged about her friend to me. As a political science major, she ranked second in the university's history of top scorers, missing number one by a half-point. The girls banded together to keep Meg from sinking into despair at the time.

"I know what you're thinking. Yes, I fell for a guy, a guy who was terminally ill. I dropped out of law school to take care of him. Then, he died. Barry died because he couldn't get the latest medical care since prior treatments had drained his financial resources. He died because the medical system ignores the poor when it comes to specialized treatments. And he was far from poor before he got sick."

"Meghan, I'm, we're sorry." My sister is embarrassingly emotional.

"Don't be. Life isn't fair, but I refuse to play the victim. I loved an excellent attorney who taught me more about law and legislature than I could have ever learned in school. He connected me to some influential players, too. I'm a better person for the experience, and thanks to him, I'll make a great lawyer.

"I'm going back to school—only a year left. Seeing all of you, well, it helps. My soul seems to blossom around you."

An awkward silence over Meghan's fate hangs like a winter's ocean mist, oppressive and chilling.

"Then, it's timely that we got back together so we can cheer you on," Blair says.

Sam places her hand on Meghan's arm. "You damn straight. Meghan will be the best lawyer ever."

"Here, here. To our lovely gal, Meghan." Debbie raises her glass, and we toast as Meghan lowers her head over the fuss that must embarrass her.

Blair changes the subject. "All right, ladies, so what can we do about a murdered animal? The poor thing will never get justice."

Sam is livid. "The puppy isn't an 'it,' Blair."

Samantha's Asian accent blends sharply with her soprano voice, projecting loudly like a territorial monkey, especially when she is excited or angry.

"All creatures are living, emotional beings, not its. Dogs and cats save people all the time. Years ago, my cat howled, which made the dog bark in my ear. I found my mom on the floor, screaming for help behind a closed door. Those animals saved her life, no doubt about it."

Debbie challenges her. "Yes, well, you are right, darlin,' but how many people see the beauty in life? Entire countries are callous toward murdering their beautiful critters. How can we expect more of a species that aborts its babies? Compared to that mindset, what the hell is a dead pup swinging in the wind?"

Meghan says, "Let's leave a woman's choice out of this conversation. But animal killings, abuse, or torture are often a sociopath's first step out, a red flag. Serial killers often begin with animals. Unfortunately, most laws don't intervene until after they kill a person."

"Then, by that standard, we are becoming a country of sociopaths." Deb is disgusted and in a mood.

Sam's emotional depth and love for animals tickle me somehow.

"I try to…you know, enlighten people back home; pets are family, not robotic pests. Besides, what punishment does an animal abuser get under U.S. laws?"

"A reprimand, maybe a fine, but the offender won't do much time," Meghan speaks as though she is ashamed of the legal system. "It depends on the state and the county. It is changing slowly, but it's different all over the country."

"Meanwhile, animals, babies, and kids live in the same world with these perpetrators unless we do something about it."

"Like what, Debs? Stand around picketing for justice, calling legislators, and waiting years to pass new laws?" Sam's accent gets thicker and more energetic the faster she talks.

Blair agrees. "Meanwhile, how many animals are

made to suffer, and how many people die at some sicko's hand by then?"

Debbie catches her second wind. "Exactly, Blair. We must find a solution now."

"I'm for that." Sam smacks the table. "Anyone else?"

Meghan nods. "Count me in for that challenge. I'll begin some legal research."

"Wait a minute, ladies, count you in for what? Again, what can four working people do? Oh, sorry, Little Sis, and a college student?" Blair asks.

Deb scrutinizes her friends. "Let's begin with our local killer. I'll research the family that owns the hanging tree. We'll meet next week, at the same time, to do something productive over a few drinks. Once we name the beast, we will better know what to do with him or her. Meanwhile, if y'all join me, we will create the change needed to benefit all animals like we talked about during the early years."

The four women were so close in college that they considered me a part of their lives, too, an extension of Blair. When my sister sent a present for my birthday, each one sent me a gift. They never met me, but that's my point. They were peas in a pod. Now, they are joining forces to solve the murder of innocence.

And I'm all in.

Chapter 4

No one prods me to attend girl's night out this week because the topic captivates me. Being a part of catching an animal killer, even in the slightest way, has me dressed and ready minutes early. But girl's night begins like the last, except we arrive earlier and score a four-top. The bar isn't nearly as crowded, and a male server ambles over —a bleached-blond-surfer type.

The ladies order stiff drinks and food this week. I'm sticking with cranberry juice. Sam studies the server, but she doesn't ask his name. She winks at Meghan again. "Too…ah… relaxed."

Meghan nods.

Debbie finishes two drinks before she moves our glasses and sets her briefcase on the table. She pulls out a folder with pages of information inside.

"Okay. Before sharing what's in this brief, I must know it will stay between us. No pillow talk. No gossiping with anyone outside our group. The report centers on an underage kid; I got it by questionable means. My point is that secrecy is essential. Y'all in?"

"With that opening, you bet I'm in." Meghan peeks at the papers Debbie is holding. Blair, Sam, and I lean our heads toward the center of the table as Debbie snaps the case closed and places it back on the floor.

I'm feeling like a covert spy, and I like it.

"All right, then. The Overmeyer's own the puppy's

hanging tree so Jack, my detective, started there. Dr. and Mrs. Overmeyer's son, Seth, is a troubled fifteen-year-old. Although they appear to be decent, loving parents, they've gone through their share of troubles with Seth since an early age —you know, school reports, neighbors.

"The report says Seth is an only child... now. Two other babies died from crib death, the certificates say, but I don't think so."

"What do you mean you don't think so?" Meghan asks.

"We thought the killer began with animals, but maybe he started with newborns."

"Oh, Debbie, that's a huge assumption." Meghan dons her legal hat. "How can you prove that?"

"You forget, girlfriend, I am rich. I can afford certain privileges like my private detective."

"Still doesn't prove a thing," Meghan whispers.

"You got this information from a reputable private eye?" Blair is awestruck, but Debbie's bank account and upbringing always charm her.

"Of course, he is highly regarded in my circles. Plus, I've known Jack for years, and I did my share of the work confirming this information. This hooligan likes to brag, but most kids stay away from him. He terrifies a few classmates who call him nuts and evil. Even teachers admit "something is off" about him. Still, he's no dummy as far as grades are concerned. I suspect he's intelligent enough to cover up any crime."

What? My ears perk up with that piece of information. Hmm. I wonder how smart? I love a credible challenge.

"My man found the pet store where they bought the

poor creature. The sales clerk remembers Dr. Overmeyer saying it was to be a gift. The poor thing ends up dead the next morning. Maybe the kid did it to vent some anger at his parents."

By the fourth drink, Debbie convinces her friends that the teen needs psychiatric care and placement far away from society. Still, they face last-call right where they had started. What will they do about it?

Sam scrunches her forehead while her tiny hands clasp tightly under her chin. "You gave this information to the police, didn't you?"

Debbie sighs. "The police are aware already. They've painted the morbid picture, but there isn't much they can do about it. They can't afford to follow Seth's every move. His parents must be in denial or, worse, scared of their son.

"Imagine Mr. Allen and the shocking view, causing him to call the police. Had he known Seth was dangerous, he might have been more discreet. Since the officers showed up to remove the pup and then went straight over to question the neighbor, he may be in danger.

"Jack insists on keeping an eye on Mr. Allen's house on his own time —that's how much he distrusts Seth. Maybe we'll catch the boy in the act of revenge since he knows who called the police."

"Meanwhile, we let the neighbor sit within Seth's reach?" Blair's voice betrays a hint of panic. "Shouldn't we warn him?" She grabs a nacho and dips it into salsa that proves too hot for her to eat.

"Ladies, again, you are speculating. There is no proof that Seth killed the animal. Deb's going about this the right way —sit and wait."

Blair shakes her head. "Well, I don't feel right about it, Meghan. Mr. Allen could be in danger; at least, a warning is in order. Sam, how do you feel about it?"

"Aiya. It depends. Is the neighbor single, married, or have any kids?"

"That's a good question." Debbie studies her notes. "For now, Mr. Allen is alone. But his wife and kids will move in next week. Hm. I wish we knew the *why* for the display of violence. Was it to spite his parents only?"

"Or as a warning to the new neighbor?" Blair asks.

Meghan shakes her head. "Again, if the boy even did it."

"Aiya. Since we can't prove anything, we should wait until the family arrives, then we say something to protect the children since Seth is so violent."

"Okay, done. My P.I. will keep an eye on Seth and Mr. Allen. All agreed?"

Outnumbered, Blair takes a deep breath. "I'm going on record as not agreeing to the wait, but I'll abide by the majority rule. I hope your P.I. knows what he's doing, Deb."

"He's an outstanding individual and the best detective around. No need to worry."

I agree with my sister about Mr. Allen and wonder if his new home has a security system.

If it doesn't, he should be very concerned.

Chapter 5

Blair curses Friday morning as she inhales her coffee.

Pfft. You have to pay to play.

Worry seeps from her pores as she mumbles about how she wishes she could warn the neighbor. "Majority rules …"

Her hangover moans and sighs irk me as she lowers the blinds, protecting her sensitive eyes from the morning sunshine.

"God, get me through this day, and I'll stop drinking so much on Thursday nights."

I remind my sister that she no longer believes in God.

"Okay, it's just an expression, Little Sis. Besides, I believe in a creator who is too big for humans to understand. I don't believe in all the religious dogma anymore."

Blair pops a few aspirins and begins her workday, scuffling out the door as though each step aches.

****

Tonight, Blair goes out on a first date but comes home early.

"What a waste of time. The man never stopped talking about himself!"

Other excuses I've heard are "no interest, no sparks; he was dull."

Too many first dates with my attractive sister do not become second dates. Chemistry is essential to her. Brains are a liability to them, I'm guessing.

"If it wasn't there, it wasn't there," she says, frowning in defeat.

The weekend passes with mundane college assignments as my only priority. I pour a glass of coconut milk before reaching for Blair's buzzing phone. It's midnight, Monday morning. Caller I.D. shows Debbie, who should know better than to call so late.

"Debbie, it's Char. Blair's in bed asleep."

"This is important, Little Sis. Wake her up, darlin'."

"She gets up early for work and told me…"

"Charlotte, she needs to hear this; take the phone to her."

Reluctantly, I tap on Blair's door, with memories of trying to wake Regena from a stupor.

"Debbie says it's extremely urgent."

"Put it on speaker, Little Sis, and set it on the table, please." She forces herself to sit up and stretch. "Good God, Debbie, do you know how late it is? Are you okay?"

"No, I'm not okay. My private investigator, Jack, he's dead."

"What? Oh, no, the one investigating, Seth?"

"Yes, the one investigating Seth. How many P. I. s do you think I employ for heaven's sake?"

"How?"

"Fire. Mr. Allen's house, you know, across from the Overmeyer's. Jack called me first and ran in to save the neighbor. I called the fire station, but it was too late. They didn't get out; they didn't make it."

"This is horrible. Did the police arrest Seth?"

"Arrest a kid at home in bed, sleeping, according to his parents?"

"Do we know it was him?" Blair asks a fair question, in my opinion.

"Good God, girlfriend. There is no way to prove it unless they find some device or accelerator that started the fire and then link it to Seth. They are investigating now. The police will question why a P.I. was in the house. The nine-one-one call-in shows my number, so I expect the authorities to contact me. If they leak my name to a reporter or whomever, I'll be next on the kid-monster list. I'm getting a concealed weapon license so I can carry it everywhere. I suggest you do the same."

"You are pinning all of this on a little boy. You're scaring me, and I don't have a gun. I wouldn't know what to do with it anyway."

"Now you sound like Meghan. I'm going with my gut on this one. We should all be scared. Buy a 22 semi-automatic —it's lightweight and perfect for a beginner. Learn how to use it. I'm leaving town for a few days, but I'll see you on Thursday night. Call the girls; let them know." Debbie doesn't bother with a goodbye.

"How am I supposed to sleep with murder and arson on my mind? I hope you can sleep, Lil Sis."

I can't answer. My heart beats like an overwound clock. My sister and her friends have stumbled upon a killer. Electricity tingles throughout my body, the likes I have never known.

As the sun rises, I'm still digesting all the facts I learned online about sociopaths, psychopaths, and arson. I weigh the data in secret, but Blair's imagination goes into overdrive before we leave for work and classes. She insists we use an old movie trick, placing a piece of scrap paper in the door so if anyone opens it, the trash will fall to the ground, betraying a violation of her condominium.

"I know this seems extreme, Charlotte. After all, Seth is only fifteen, and he doesn't know our names or addresses. I'm probably being silly. I won't bother Sam and Meghan with this latest news …yet."

I keep quiet, brushing off Blair's oddness as a full day of classes awaits me. The hint of danger in my life excites me as I breeze through each subject. I'm not convinced that a fifteen-year-old can't be dangerous.

Blair's subconscious must feel the same way because she texts me: "Meet me at Shooters. Four o'clock." That means Blair is leaving work early. Just how paranoid has she become?

I arrive at Shooters in time to see Blair purchase two 22s. She doesn't ask if I want a gun; She assumes I do and asks for my license so that each weapon is registered individually. The manager's name tag says Hunter. I enjoy the irony as he files the papers.

"Why don't you stay and learn how to use the weapon at the indoor firing range behind the store?"

I'm glad Blair agrees because I itch to begin. Hunter leads the way to the building, which is almost empty at this time of day.

"All right, ladies. Let me adjust this area for broad daylight. Now, we can see. The first thing to learn about your weapon is how to remove and load the clip." He shows us that part. "The clip holds the bullets. Always store the gun without the clip."

He inserts the clip only to press a tiny lever that releases it. Easy enough. The mechanism gives Blair trouble, but she manages to get it right the third time.

"It's alright, Blair, you have a typical case of nerves.

Practice makes perfect. Now, we'll learn how to load. This gun doesn't require a special bullet, as some do. Okay? Watch how I load the clip."

Hunter shows us the correct direction of the bullets, loading them into the top of the clip. Once he completes that step, he inserts the clip into the gun. "Okay. I want you to remove the clip."

Blair trips the lever, removing it clumsily while I've already finished.

"Good. Now take all the bullets out."

My fingers seem adept at the piecework. Blair drops a bullet to the ground.

"Okay, ladies, load it."

Blair's fingers shake as she inserts the first bullet.

"Good. You are loading it in the correct direction."

I'm impressed with Hunter's gentleness with Blair. Again, I finish while my sister is still loading. She gives me an exasperated murmur.

"Okay. Place the clip in the gun." We place it correctly. "Now, check for a bullet in the chamber. Good job. Remember, I want you to practice loading and unloading every day, remembering to check the chamber. It should become second nature to you. If you gals are ready, we'll practice shooting. Put on your headphones and protective eyewear. That's right. Here's how to line up your site."

My sister insists that he shoot first, which senseless, but Hunter's action seems to ease her nerves.

"Okay, Blair. Your turn." Hunter pushes a button that brings the target in closer. "Line up the site. Squeeze. Fire." She misses the entire target in her first few shots. "Blair, if you want to improve, keep your eyes open. Also, don't yank your finger back; ease it and squeeze it gently."

Success. She hits the mark in the stomach and smiles.

"There ya go!" He says, truly happy for her.

She adapts to the feel of a gun in her hand, although I doubt Blair will ever feel comfortable with it. But a loaded weapon empowers me. When the instructor announces it is my turn, I nod.

"I'm ready."

"Okay. Just remember, few women hit the target their first time out. Where men like the weight and the power of a gun, women, for the most part, react a bit squeamishly. I always remind them that if they don't want to be a victim, they need to learn the ins and outs of any weapon. Let me bring in the target."

"No! Leave it." I tire of his patronizing voice. I'll show him how fair and weak I am. I concentrate, squeeze the trigger, and am thrilled that my shot has neutered the dummy.

"Ouch. You hit it, Charlotte. Good for you. I'm glad I'm not that guy." Hunter is both surprised and impressed.

Blair laughs. "Good job, Little Sis. I've met a couple of guys that needed castration. Oh, only kidding, Hunter."

We practice for a half-hour and thank our teacher. Blair will share the wonder of my first shot with the girls. In turn, they will congratulate me and hoot and holler at my lucky bullseye. No one needs to know I chose that exact spot.

****

As we near our front door, Blair tenses until she sees the undisturbed paper.

I assure her, "There's no need to be scared."

To her credit, she swallows her terror. "I'm glad I bought the gun and learned how to shoot it, but I still feel like a wimp. Thank goodness I'm not alone here anymore. I'm so glad you're with me, Little Sis."

I force a smile. Blair is alone in the cowardly department. Still, it's nice to know my sister is honest, even if she is weak. She not only locks the door behind us but slides the chain in place and pushes a chair under the knob. Emotionally, she needs extra protection at night, forgetting that her condominium is on the second floor.

I try to reassure her. "No one is going to climb up the outside of the building and get through the sliding doors with its security bar."

My words don't make a dent. To be safe, she insists we tug a sizable decorative planter under the windowsill next to the sliding door. Our intended murderer would surely knock it down or fall in it and cause a racket.

"The noise will wake us in time to grab a knife or bat until the gun is safely in the apartment."

"We don't own a bat."

"Oh, right. But we do own a knife or two."

"Steak knives."

"Well, there you go, the right size for a lady to hide under the pillow." Blair gets two, insisting I take one.

One shooting lesson makes her more afraid than before. I'm concerned she could accidentally shoot me when we bring the guns home.

Chapter 6

Charlotte

Blair paces back and forth in the kitchen like a caged tiger; I try to ignore it.

"Maybe I should call Sam and Meghan about the fire. Debbie wanted me to, but I don't want to worry them."

Knowing she won't be able to wait until Thursday's girl's night, I give her another minute. Sure enough, she Skypes Sam and Meghan a day late. I nibble on a stale bran muffin while listening to the conference call. When Blair tells them about the fire, Sam is livid.

"That killer graduated to humans already."

I peer over Blair's shoulder. Sam reminds me of a dormant volcano. It's there, little at first, but it grows fast. Sometimes, her silence shakes the ground; it is a real problem when it starts to blow. An eruption is near as Samantha's face glows from the blood rush; her eyes steam in high definition.

But Meghan reacts to the news with urgency and a level head. "I've contemplated GNO all weekend long."

"Wait. What is NO?" Sam asks curtly.

"It's GNO, Sam. Pronounced 'no' for no more animal abuse and our girls' night out."

"Oh, Meghan, very clever. I like it." Sam slowly defuses.

"I do, too, Megs," Blair says.

"Sam, understand that I'm on top of it. I've thought about animal abuse and outlined a few procedures and laws that I'll present to local and state legislators I've befriended. Oh, and you will all be happy to know I re-applied to complete my law degree in Jacksonville."

GNO has encouraged her to get on with life. The possibility that an animal killer had jumped to the next level must support her decision. We acknowledge Meghan's proactive move with positive, approving responses.

"What do we do about our no-good, rat-bastard murderer, Meghan?" Sam is heating up again.

"I'm certain the police are on the case. Let's do one step at a time."

Blair changes the topic, telling everyone about our experience at the shooting range and bragging about my first shot. That brings a weak round of approval. Blair mouths to me: *They hate guns.* The cyber meeting ends, but it irritates me. Skyping with Meghan and Sam is more lateral than productive.

My sister, still in defense mode, insists that we become physically stronger. She is not one to procrastinate, so she signs us up for our first yoga class on Wednesday evening. Yoga is a stretch for me, no pun intended. But I agree to try one class for the experience.

The community center's oversized room is filling up quickly. Although signing the attendance list isn't mandatory, Blair wants to check the names of attendees. She stares at the signatures, pulls me over, and points.

On the list is the name Trish Overmeyer.

"Couldn't be, could it?" I whisper over a fantastic opportunity. Everyone is warming up. Who looks like a

Trish Overmeyer? Our eyes scan the room as it fills with colorful yoga mats that form a fascinating mosaic.

Blair introduces us to the yoga instructor. "Hi. I'm Blair Toiffler, and this is my sister, Charlotte. I'm looking forward to your class."

"Nice to meet you, too. I'm Lucy. Are you new to Ujjayi Pranayama?"

"Yes. Men dominate my workplace. They can be pushy, so I tense up and sometimes forget about breathing."

"You'd be surprised how many people tell me the same thing. This class will help you in many ways. Ujjayi, diaphragmatic breathing, forces oxygen deep into your lungs. But I'll explain all that at the start. Meanwhile, you're welcome to warm up."

"Uh, I tend to be a little shy. I noticed an Overmeyer on the guest list; I met her once. Do you know where she is?"

Wow, my sister can pull off the innocent act. I'm impressed with her ability to deceive.

"Trish. Yes, she is a Yoga devotee and always takes a spot in the back of my class by the door. If you want, I can re-introduce you."

"No, she may not remember me —that would be awkward. We better warm up." Blair winks at me and nods to the back of the room.

My heart flutters, wondering about Trish Overmeyer. There, in the corner, with dark circles under her eyes, her mouth sealed shut, frowning lips, worry lines, and unkempt hair —it must be her. I nudge Blair in the right direction.

"Excuse me, are you Trish?" The woman reacts like a deer caught in headlights.

"I'm sorry; I didn't mean to startle you. Lucy said you attend regularly, and we're new. It would help if we worked next to someone who knew what they were doing. Do you mind?" Blair plops down her mat before Trish can answer.

Seth's mother lies flat on her back, legs up against the wall. Blair copies her position.

"Am I doing this position correctly?"

Trish turns her head toward Blair and nods.

The first session is unusually long since it begins with a history of Ujjayi Pranayama. We sit in a lotus position as the teacher starts the class.

"The Sanskrit word Pranayama comes from Prana (life energy) and Ayana (to extend, draw out)."

Blair and I try not to stare at Trish, but what are the odds? Before I know it, the teaching process begins.

"To create the Ujjayi Breath, one must constrict the back of the throat, like the constriction made when speaking in a whisper. Although there is a constriction of the throat, the Ujjayi Breath flows in and out through the nostrils, with the lips remaining gently closed. Watch my example."

This kind of breathing, which is not as easy as it appears, could benefit my energy levels; it interests me. I lose track of time while practicing breathing correctly and copying poses. I'm drawn back to awareness when the door next to us opens.

"Mom. It's time. I've waited long enough, and you know I don't like waiting."

Trish jumps up, rolling her mat. "Seth, it isn't nice to interrupt-"

A tall bush of orange hair framing a pale white, acne-sprinkled face scowls at his mother. He could have been any ordinary teen until he grabbed Trish's elbow, causing her to wince.

"Seth, you're hurting me." Seth kicks open the door and pulls out his mother, letting the door slam shut.

"Little Sis, did we just see what we saw?" Blair whispers.

"You saw it." Anger grows inside me. I had never treated Regena that way, and she deserved it more than Trish, the doormat. I struggle to focus on the instructor's calm voice and do what she says…breathe while remembering each second of the scene I witnessed between a killer and his mother.

Thankfully, Blair drives home in silence. What is there to say? By the time she readies for bed, her mood lightens. "I certainly have news to share at the next GNO."

We say goodnight, but I toss and turn between dreams and wakefulness. In a dream, Seth and my mother share lead roles. When I can't stand their gruff voices anymore, I pull out a machine gun and mow them down. I wake up soaked in sweat. The same dream captures me again, with a slight variation in the scenario, but it always ends the same way.

Chapter 7

Charlotte

Deb holds a table in the corner, away from the noisy music at Sandy Bottoms.

"Debbie, I've been worried about you. Where have you been?"

"Hi, Blair, Charlotte. Taking a few refresher courses."

"For teaching?"

"No. For surviving. I earned a black belt in my teens, but I'm rusty. I wanted a reminder on a few points."

Hm. How good is she?

Sam and Meghan arrive together.

"I hear music." Sam is excited but too short to see over the crowd. "Is it Karaoke?"

"No," her friends reply together.

"It's a country theme tonight, not your favorite." Meghan softens the blow.

Sam's face scrunches with disappointment.

"What's the latest news?" Meghan asks Debbie.

"After I called Blair, I flew to the vineyard to visit my Sensei. He's getting my Karate skills back up to speed."

Imagining a match with Debbie interests me, but I doubt if a few days of practice would advance her to my level. Thanks to Blair funding my lessons during my teens, I'm certain I could take her down.

"Jack's funeral is tomorrow. I'm going; I wonder if Seth will turn up to gloat. Mr. Allen's coworkers scheduled a memorial for him the following day. He's new here, so there won't be many in attendance; I'm going there, too. I feel responsible, somehow."

"That's ridiculous. You had nothing to do with anyone's death."

"Thanks, Meghan, but I do want to pay my respects. Seth might make an appearance for the new guy, too. Pretty stupid if he does, but he is a teenager. You were right, Blair. We should have warned the new guy about Seth right away."

Blair shakes her head. "This is one time I wish I had been wrong."

Sam lets out a list of superlatives that would make a sailor cringe. Finally, she gets control of herself while I hide my amusement. "That little shit. He's the one to blame, not you or us, Debbie. We can't let that turd get away with this; no, we can't."

Blair says, "Debbie, if the police talk to you, will you mention our names too?"

For the first time, I am ashamed of my big sister — coward. So, what if they have our names?

"Blair, you're exceptionally paranoid," Meghan says.

Sam shakes her finger. "Hm. Maybe not, Megs. Maybe the kid psycho knows someone hired the detective. Maybe he hopes Debbie and friends show up." Sam becomes animated. "He could be waiting to slit your throat," she says while enacting the slit across her own throat.

Good grief, the paranoia is catching.

"Ladies, get a grip. Files were still locked up in Jack's office. I destroyed my folder in the shredder, just in case. Seth set fire to the neighbor's house, not realizing he would get lucky and kill two at once. No one ever says that evil doesn't pay well."

"But what about your call to nine-one-one? Haven't they investigated your connection?" Blair asks.

"I turned off my phone for a few days and got home late last night. No big deal if the law sees my number. I'll tell them the truth; Jack and I were friends, so he called me first."

"I'm glad I bought a twenty-two for Char and me. It's a good start for protection."

Sam's eyes balloon as though she sees a ghost. "Aiya. Guns scare me."

"Even when you realize there's a crazy teen loose in our town?" Debbie is fearless.

"Yes, crazy fuckers everywhere." Sam's voice shakes.

"Uh, that's why I bought the gun, and after what I saw last night, I'm glad I did."

All eyes are on my sister. "Okay, Blair, spill."

"Minus the drama? Well, Char and I took our first yoga class last night, and you won't believe who was there."

The trio's ears perk just a bit.

Meghan urges her on. "Go on, Blair."

"Trish Overmeyer."

"Seth's mother?" The three conspirators gasp all at once.

Blair nods. "I know. Can you imagine? But that's not all." She tells them the whole story.

"The prick." Sam clenches her teeth. "I wonder how

much longer he will let Trish live."

"Y'all are jumping to conclusions, outrageous conclusions about this boy. There is no proof he killed his neighbor or the P.I.; now y'all think he might kill his mother." Meghan's furrowed high forehead betrays her frustration.

"Wrong, Megs. The investigator deemed the fire arson." Debbie licks the salt off her glass rim. The margarita is gone, and only the salt remains. "Who's our server tonight, and why am I sitting in front of an empty glass?"

"Well, it may have been arson, but you don't know if Seth started it?" Meghan insists.

"How do you catch a murdering brat if his parents lie to protect him?" My sister has a point.

"You don't," Debbie says, chomping on a piece of ice, an action very unlike her. "The killer boy grows up to be a murdering man, and maybe, by then, he'll get sloppy. Eventually, the police may find him. Let's hope somebody does something soon to stop him first."

I dare to express my opinion. "Sam, you could hack into his system and keep an eye on him. See whom he talks to … "

Meghan cuts me off. "You know better than that. Hacking is illegal."

Sam winks, agreeing with me, but she takes it a step further. "Charlotte is right. Better yet, someone needs to take that boy out before he kills again." She picks up her twizzle stick and chews on it like a toothpick. Debbie nods, but Blair is appalled, shaking her head.

"I don't know what is scarier…having a psycho loose or a vigilante who thinks he is above the law."

"He? What makes you think the vigilante would be

a man? A woman can kill as well as a man, just sayin'." Sam takes a long sip of her brandy Alexander. "Why do you all look shocked? I don't think erasing a murderer should be against the law."

Meghan shakes her head. "Eliminating, not erasing, Sam. But it's not how the American system works—innocent until proven guilty. No proof exists yet. The law follows procedures to avoid mistakes."

"I don't think Sam means regular cases that the court system resolves easily," Debbie says. "She means oddball situations like this one. For some reason, Seth, a "person of interest," evades the law continually. Meanwhile, there's a world full of Seth's, and they enjoy easy pickings thanks to our weak laws."

"Exactly, Debbie. Thanks to the Internet, these freaks stay in touch with one another, sharing their techniques, their dirty little secrets," Sam says.

Blair unwisely switches to a beer. "Although I understand your points, really, I do, you must agree that vigilantes become murderers and maybe not just once in their lives. The way the world is today, they won't be satisfied with one victim, I bet."

"Vigilantes don't take out victims. They take out the predators, the hunters who make victims. But I could name a few more souls who could use a quick exit or a good lesson." Debbie is focused.

"Like who?" Sam sports an eager smile.

"How about Ken Lay and Jeff Skillings, who took down the corporate giant Enron? People lost their pensions because of them. Ken Lay died of a heart attack before he served any time. Hmm, at least the news reported his death as a heart attack. Skillings got a short sentence in a light-security prison. How about the Wall

Street thieves who enjoy their golden parachutes?"

"Aiya. Execution better suits that Ponzi man, Madoff, than the jail time he got." Sam makes the sign of a slit throat again. "He ruined a lot of lives."

"You can't murder people because they're greedy. We are a nation of laws, after all." Meghan is frustrated with her friends and takes a large gulp of her martini.

"Who's talking about murdering?" Blair is tipsy before everyone else. "This is hypothetical, ladies, but it sure is an emotional subject."

"Blair, you tell me: if some bastard took out Little Sis and got off on a technicality, you wouldn't avenge her?" Sam scores a goal in my mind.

My sister is speechless for a second. "Well, there was a time I would have tried forgiveness as the Dominicans taught me. But of course, I would use every avenue of the law to avenge Little Sis's death and not go crazy about it. I mean, we are a civilized people."

Sam nudges me. "How about you, Char? If someone murders Blair, what would you do?"

I stare at my sister sitting there. My mind forgets the Dominican sisters, whose ideals center on justice and love, who encourage their students to adopt the same stance. I would choose to apply the Old Testament teaching.

"God said 'eye for an eye.' I'd put a bullet right through the perp's heart." A tingle possesses my spine and zips through the rest of my body.

"That's what I'm talking about. If the law doesn't work, do something about it," Sam gloats.

Debbie says, "Wait a minute. I can understand the passion of a retribution killing, but I must agree with Blair on this one. I'm against killing a thief, no matter how many people suffer from it. They need to be punished in a more creative way, like a hacker could do. Death is too good for them. Instead, make them poor overnight with nowhere to turn. That's a financial alternative of an eye for an eye. Still illegal but less violent."

"Oh, Debbie, what a good idea—what fun. Most hackers couldn't touch their billions, but I could break through their encryptions and walls. It would be wonderful to see those calculating, greedy princes or princesses end up broke and homeless," Sam says seriously.

Meghan, hearing the unlawful comments, switches to water. She can't get her pro-law point across.

Debbie winks. "Just how good are you, sweet Sam?"

"Aiya. I'm a genius." Sam's statement has no ego attached to it. "CIA wants me, FBI wants me, everybody tries to hire me. But I need a life, too. My government job is fine. But if I wanted, I could take care of the greedy sons-of-the-bitches."

"Too bad the public seems unworried about all the injustices occurring. They go on, maybe a little grouchier, but no one does anything about the assholes," Debbie says.

"Because there are not enough coronaries to keep others from doing the same thing. "

Everyone seems confused as I chuckle to myself.

Meghan shakes her head. "You meant something other than coronaries, Sam. Maybe corollaries or consequences?"

"Aiya. Okay, both."

Blair seems eager to change the subject once again. "Did you see the photo today of African elephants murdered for their tusks?"

Meghan responds gratefully for her tactic. "Awful. Commoners in the Far East still think tusks are medicinal, so poachers murder them to get rich overnight."

"Hey, I thought governments protected elephants now."

"Well, they try, Sam, but poachers make their way into the park and have at it." Meghan won't be able to soothe her over this topic.

Debbie says, "Why don't they place soldiers or volunteers on duty with AK 47s and place signs all around the park that say, 'poachers, shot on sight. No excuses accepted.' Now that's protection. Instead, poachers might get arrested after the kill and hit with a reprimand like our local crazy boy."

I finally speak because the subject is important to me. "They already do. I saw an article about Caramba National Park in Central Africa, in the Congo. Kony and his militia attacked the park, killing many of the guards. Then they slaughtered a family of elephants, even babies that didn't have tusks yet.

"After that, park security guards were trained in guerrilla tactics and supplied with automatic weapons. Still, the tusks are so valuable that Kony attacked again anyway."

"What the hell for?" Debbie's face burns red.

"Here's a strange irony. Kony wants to take over Uganda. He needs money to accomplish that, and Ivory is like gold in the Far East."

"Aiya. That bullshit hypocrisy." Sam garners looks from the closest table to ours.

"Why do people want that much ivory?" My sister

is clueless.

"They believe it has medicinal purposes and is an aphrodisiac."

Debbie rolls her eyes. "You're kidding. What's the matter over there? Can't anyone get it up naturally anymore?"

Sam turns purple. I think she might burst. She does, laughing hysterically. "Good joke, Debbie. Why do you think I stay in America?"

Meghan ignores the humor, looking pale after hearing the news. "What's wrong with this sickening world? It's humiliating to be human."

Debbie half-stands on the rungs of her bar stool. "It's only embarrassing when we sit back and let it happen. Ladies, I suggest we stop living our safe, comfortable lives and start walking the fine line. With my money and our weekly meetings, we could make some changes, safeguard our community, animals, and families."

Alcohol loosens the tongue, and this night, GNO seals its motivation…justice—first case: Seth Overmeyer, my favorite teenage psychopath.

Debbie finally sits down. "I say we continue weekly meetings to figure out a plan of action starting locally. But for now, there's one hour left, so let's wear off the injustices that soil our brain and act like a table of party gals instead."

Meghan shakes her head. She deserves to let loose but knows when too much alcohol is too much. Although she and I come from opposite ends of the argument, I respect her steadfastness. My sister and her friends are formidable as a group. Even though the bar is full of men, none approach our table. Typical. The group of intellectual beauties frightens the average male.

As though she reads my mind, Blair speaks up. "Debbie, can't we meet where the class of men is a little more progressive? You know, where having a brain isn't a liability. I'm tired of this sad selection."

"A liability? Us?" Debbie laughs. "You mean a country club atmosphere with educated and successful men, oh and women too, Sam."

Sam plays both sides of the team. She loves love, whether it comes from a man or a woman. It is easy for her to be in love with more than one person at a time, but Blair says her standards are very high.

"Thanks, girlfriend. This switch-hitter will be happy with anyone but these drunken yuppies."

Blair says, "But we need to talk without interruption if we're going to fix anything."

"A girl's night out is a good cover for us and any clandestine solutions we come up with. But it's difficult to decide when to start the meeting and end it officially. Maybe we should keep playtime and meeting time separate. That's my opinion," Meghan says.

Debbie nods, "True. We started girl's night out as playtime, but now we're trying to accomplish something. I'll tell you what, ladies. Save Thursday night for GNO, where we find solutions to current problems, and you can use my club membership on Saturdays. Hob knob with some money makers, then. If they don't take care of the bill, I will."

Debbie acts as if her generosity is no big deal. Sam, Meghan, and Blair take a second to reach a consensus. "That's a generous offer we can't refuse. Thank you." Meghan speaks for all.

"Thank you is unnecessary. It's about time we shed

complacency. Now turn around slowly and feast your eyes on the pretty boys who just walked in."

Sam laughs. "Haven't you developed gaydar yet? Make room, ladies, and get ready to dance off the alcohol." Sam invites the latecomers to last-call.

Perfect timing—the DJ plays an oldie but goodie, YMCA.

As the crowd enjoys the arm movements, I cringe. This isn't my idea of fun or progress.

I need a plan.

Chapter 8

Friday morning, Blair rolls over, cursing the alarm and whimpering so loudly that I hear her in the kitchen.

"I did it again. Oh, my stomach."

Big sister is bound to muddle through another day with her head pounding and stomach rumbling. Thankfully, her genius for numbers remains unaffected by the last hour of a chug fest. I wonder how Debbie, the practiced drinker, feels today and how Meghan and Sam manage.

Witnessing their weekly physical abuse has me assessing my health. I decide to improve my strength by joining a local gym. I allow one cranberry juice and substitute it with Evian to cut calories later. Blair's crowd provides enough entertainment, but I want to understand the facts clearly while they drink.

****

Friday evening, Blair comes home from a date even earlier than the week before. She kicks off her pumps and plops down on the couch.

"Two hours of sheer torture. It turns out this guy thinks he's the judge and jury of the world. I never would have guessed him to be a bigot. Finally, I told him, I'm sorry this isn't working for me, and I don't think it's working for you either."

She contributed to the bill and got up, leaving the man to finish his meal alone.

Blair is frustrated waiting for her prince, and I hope her luck will change at Amelia Island Resort and Yacht Club for both our sakes. I tire of her lamenting and could use more alone time in the condo.

****

Debbie meets us for an early bird dinner on Saturday night. "Hey. A young start to the night might provide more prospects, girlfriends. Some fellows have been on the water or the golf course all day and won't last long. Fresh air does that."

We sit in a lovely room decorated with latticework on sandy-colored walls overlooking the ocean. The tables, covered with a simple white tablecloth, display seafoam-colored dinnerware. An artistically folded napkin sits on the top plate, and an abundance of silverware sits on each side. Start from the outside, I remember reading.

Debbie orders a bottle of wine for the table, but as we wait, champagne arrives instead.

The server explains, "The table on your far left hopes you will accept this bottle of champagne."

"Accepted." Debbie smiles and waves without concern for anyone else's opinion. "Come on, ladies, remember, this is a fun time." She motions for the five men to come over.

I am not pleased. Curiosity about the seafood brought me with Blair's insistence, but it's time for me to vacate this scene.

Debbie bubbles. "Thank you for your generosity, gentlemen. I see you haven't ordered yet. Why don't we move to a larger table and enjoy dinner together?"

A mustached, buzz-cut blond speaks up quickly. "That's the best idea I've heard all day, ladies." The rest

49

of his entourage agrees.

While the servers set up a ten-top, Sam laughs. "Debbie, where have you been all my life?"

Debbie isn't shy; she's the typical mover and shaker. While Blair plays relationship roulette, and Meghan licks her wounds, and Sam plays both sides of the fence, Debbie lives life her way with never a dull moment. The best part is that she includes as many people as possible; her energy seems endless and unbreakable. Everyone adores her for it.

While thinking of the right moment to leave this party, I study impromptu matchmaking. Instantly, Blair connects with Harry, an accountant, and Meghan with William, a public defender. Sam struggles with attractions between the local news anchor, Frederick, and the female bartender whose low-cut sweater flaunts an ample breast.

Sam tickles me. Her passion for animals and relationships also open an understanding and permission within me. It is okay with Sam to be Sam. Contrary to what my late mother thought, I'm beginning to feel the same about myself. I'm not a freak. I just am.

Meanwhile, Debbie enamors the married Greek; wedding rings never bother her, according to Blair. Debbie says, "If it isn't me, it would be someone else. Besides, I'm taken too…almost."

As the only male left approaches me, I spring out of my seat and say my goodbyes. "Sorry, I have a headache that won't quit. I'll call a cab, Blair, pop some aspirin, and go to bed. No need to leave your dinner on my account."

I had agreed to attend this evening but not to hook up. That's a dealbreaker.

"I've never known you to have a headache. If you're sure you'll be okay …"

"It's fine, Blair, take your time, but please, when you come home, don't wake me. Let me sleep for once. I could use a full night's sleep."

"Aiya. A night without blaring Broadway music is important. You let her sleep," Sam says, pointing her finger. "And buy headphones. Music sounds even better, then." Sam winks at me.

Blair blushes. "Yes, I understand. Okay, I'll see you in the morning."

****

The night is mine. Sam isn't the only geek in the group. As usual, I sit with my laptop and find Seth online.

****

I whip up scrambled eggs and pour a mug of bold coffee while Blair snores. She needs more sleep than I do, hibernating on weekends like a bear in winter, while I only require a few hours of rest despite last night's fabricated protest.

Waiting for her to awaken, I unfold our local paper that headlines:

Local Boy Commits Suicide.

Dr. and Mrs. Overmeyer return home to discover their son dead. Seth L. Overmeyer, age fifteen, was found Sunday morning. Officials say he died from a self-inflicted gunshot wound.

Seth attended Amelia High School and was an honor student. Funeral services will be private.

The article continues, providing information on teen

suicides in the county and giving parents a list of signs of depression and suicidal tendencies. The headline will surely warrant a Skype session, but I hesitate to wake up Blair.

"I smell coffee." My sister shuffles into the kitchen, grabbing a bottle of aspirin from on top of the fridge.

"You'll want to see the headline in this morning's paper. Brace yourself."

"What do you mean?" She wipes her bed head away from her eyes. "Oh, my God."

Blair stands there, reading the entire article before she gazes at me in shock. I pour her coffee as she sets up a call.

"I'm sorry to wake you all so early."

"Aiya. Do you know what time it is?" Sam moans.

"Girlfriends, have you seen the paper?"

"Please tell me I'm still dreaming," Debbie mumbles.

"Don't hang up on me. It's about Seth Overmeyer."

"Aiya. Not first thing on a Sunday."

"It must be important; give her a chance." Meghan sounds wide awake and interested.

"The newspaper must have fit in the column just before printing. Seth—he killed himself."

No one reacts. A few seconds of dead silence fills the air.

"Did you hear me? Are y'all still there?"

Each friend responds. "Yes, I hear you."

Debbie sounds the most shocked. "You said Seth is dead, right?"

"Yes. According to the paper, he committed suicide."

"He couldn't have," Debbie yawns.

"Debbie, wake up. It's on the front page of today's paper."

"They're wrong…maybe… maybe, I'm wrong. Seth's profile doesn't fit suicide. He wouldn't have killed himself. It's too early to think, but maybe someone got rid of him and made it look like a suicide."

"Really?" Blair squirms. "Who would do that? It wasn't … well, it wasn't one of us, right?"

"Oh, hell's bells! Don't say anything like that ever again, especially online. Engage the brain, girlfriend," Debbie fumes. "Although someone did the world a favor, I wonder who that someone is; I'd love to shake their hand."

"He was a kid, and no one proved he did anything wrong."

"Meghan, he was a monster, not a kid—I doubt any psychiatric facility could have changed him. I'll Google the article in a few minutes. Let's attend Seth's funeral, too. Talk to you later." Debbie hangs up.

"Me too."

"Me three."

"Char, did we see what we thought?" Blair asks. "Did we watch without judgment and form a fair conclusion, or did our preconceived ideas transfer to imagine a killer when Seth grabbed his mother? Maybe he was only an obnoxious teenager who overstepped his bounds, as many teens do."

My sister sounds like Meghan. She re-runs the scene again.

"Seth sounded angry. Did his mother leave because she was afraid, or was she trying to avoid a scene? Had he hurt his mother purposely, or did she have an arm that was already sore from an unrelated event, and it hurt to the touch?"

My sister reaches to rub her neck, something she does when frustrated. "Innocent until proven guilty. But I wonder if he left a note?"

She wonders if there is a suicide note.

I wonder if anyone will cry at his funeral.

Chapter 9

Blair, Debbie, and I crash Seth's private graveside funeral, which is being held in a park-like setting filled with weeping willows and multi-colored flowering shrubs. Everyone carries umbrellas as black clouds hang low, looking ready to burst. We spy with a clear view from behind the parents and relatives, who form a horseshoe around the rabbi while thunder rumbles.

The rabbi says a few words. I sense he knows little about Seth. Judaism abhors suicide unless they find a reason that includes mental problems. Seth qualifies.

Mr. and Mrs. Overmeyer wear dark sunglasses, but Trish's lower lip trembles as she wipes away tears that slip past the shades. Her grief seems ridiculous to me. The boy killed her newborns and neighbors. His future would have involved more heartache. Pfft. The parents should celebrate.

Debbie nudges Blair as Doctor Overmeyer grabs his wife's elbow and pushes it away from her face. I can't read her mind. Does she think Dr. Overmeyer is the abusive one or that he doesn't like competition from his son? Or was Seth abused and turned into an abuser? There is no telling what the girls think, but there are no excuses. Even if the parents are the source of Seth's abnormalities, their son is what he is or *was*—evil.

As Trish Overmeyer steps forward to place a single yellow rose on her son's coffin, she falls to her knees.

"No, Seth. Seth." The mother plays the bereaved victim while the doctor scans those around him, seemingly embarrassed by his wife's behavior. He bends down as she claws at the dirt mound and picks her up as the casket lowers.

"Trish, it's done now. It's over. Time for us to go home, sweetheart."

There it is again: the elbow thing. The physical pain he inflicts brings Trish out of her funk. Her lips purse again as he whispers into her ear and squeezes her elbow. She winces and nods as her husband supports her body weight to the parking lot, helping her into the car. They peel off, leaving Seth inside an expensive coffin.

The stupid punk is where he belongs.

Debbie nudges Blair. "Did you see the doctor spot us? He stared at us for a while."

"Sort of, but it's hard to tell what he was looking at with those mirrored sunglasses on."

"He was trying to figure us out until Trish collapsed. I bet we'll be seeing him sometime in the future."

"Don't say that. You know I'm chicken shit. I don't want him lurking around my house." A black vortex of negativity captures my sister.

"You read too many spy novels. But one person did take pictures."

"Who brings cameras to a funeral?"

"You see that white Optima?" Debbie nods toward a car parked on the lane closest to the gravesite. "There's a man behind the wheel who snapped photos the whole time—probably an undercover police officer. He'll research and find out who we are."

"Great, so what do we tell him when he comes calling?" Blair's voice sounds panicked as clouds accumulate overhead; a few sporadic raindrops plop on our umbrellas as people rush to their cars.

"Tell him the truth –you're my friend. You came to Seth's funeral to support me. Char came to support you. Don't say any more. Don't say any less."

"And why did you come?"

"I haven't figured that out yet, but I'll think of something fast because we're about to have company."

Blair inhales deeply. "Oh, dear. Oh, my. You're my friend. Okay, I can do this."

"Ladies."

A plainclothes officer, tall and muscle-bound, struts toward us. I've heard Blair's opinion about this kind of man: "No man can have all that going on. Bet he turns out to be Dudley Do-Right in the brain department."

Dudley flashes a badge. "I'm Detective Reece. I'm investigating Seth's death. Would y'all mind if I ask you a few questions?"

"Sure thing, Mr. Handsome, fire away." Debbie winks slowly, full of self-assurance.

"All right, then." He clears his throat and turns to Blair. "Mind telling me how you knew Seth Overmeyer?"

"I don't. I mean, I never met Seth."

"You go to funerals of people you don't know?"

"No. Yes, I do because Debbie didn't want to go alone; she asked me to go with her. She's…we're friends…that's why I came, and my sister goes where I go."

"Now, Blair, don't be nervous with the detective. She gets shaken up at funerals on TV, too; don't take it personally, Officer. You see, I didn't know Seth, but I knew the private eye who died in the fire across the street from him—a friend of mine. I went to his funeral yesterday.

"Anyway, first, the new neighbor's house burned down, with him and my friend in it, and now the boy across the street committed suicide. Interesting, but tragic, don't you think?" Debbie fails to get a rise out of the detective. "So, you know what they say: Curiosity killed the cat. And here we are... meow."

Dudley struggles to contain a smile that begins to form at the corners of his mouth.

Debbie presses her point. "I don't suppose you know if one thing has to do with the other? I mean, one fire and one suicide within a week across the street from each other."

"Ms. ...."

"Debbie. You can call me Debbie."

"No, actually, I'll need your last names."

Debbie quit hitting on the detective long enough for him to fill out a white pad the same size as his mitt-like hand. "Thank you. We make it a point to investigate what appear to be non-related events, but we don't discuss our work. That's what *detectives* do."

I suppose he doesn't appreciate Debbie's patronizing.

"Ladies, I won't see you again if all your information checks out. Good afternoon."

"Now, that would be a terrible thing, the not 'seeing' you part. You have my number if you change your mind." Shamelessly, Debbie sends another wink.

The officer nods at Debbie but smiles at Blair, blushes, then hustles toward his car.

Blair is miffed. "Did you ever stop to think that maybe I'd be interested in him?"

"Don't get your panties in a twist. Superman doesn't interest me. I wanted him to walk away with a straightforward experience with us. It doesn't hurt to have the police officers on our side."

"A detective, not an ordinary cop. Still, he wasn't your type, but he sure was mine. Strong, well-spoken, understated, unlike your performance. Anyway, my knees knocked the whole time he asked questions. Let's have some wine."

Blair must be relieved that the detective is gone, but I sense she's also disappointed.

"That a girl. You're speaking my language."

We duck inside Debbie's SUV as the deluge begins.

During brunch at a local restaurant and three glasses of wine later, Blair speaks about Seth's death with concern, as though he were a relative.

"It's hard to believe someone stepped over the line, maybe even pulled the trigger for him. I doubt we would ever have the guts to do something like that."

"Again? Read my lips; don't say stuff like that. We talked about doing something about Seth but not to him. Sam and Meghan? Sam won't do anything more than talk if that's what you're implying, and Meghan's never even had a speeding ticket, let alone encourage a death.

"We're all together in solving this mystery, aren't we? It is odd how the kid gave us a mission, and now, we have to figure out if his death was really a suicide or if someone made it look like a suicide."

Blair wonders aloud. "Strange. I mean, it started with an animal killing. Are we sure he even did that?"

"I wonder if any other neighborhood pets disappeared. I could ask my new detective."

"Well, if another of your detectives dies, I'm

changing my name and moving somewhere far away."

"Don't run away from life, no matter how dangerous it gets. You play the part handed to you no matter what happens."

There you go.

"All right, Debbie, no lectures. Besides, I'm exaggerating, maybe. But the four of us get together for old time's sake, and next thing we know, we're on the periphery of a double murder and a possible suicide."

Debbie laughs.

"Never a dull moment, right?" My sister slurs her words.

I'm glad that I possess the willpower that Blair lacks. I am not bound to food, drugs, or people.

****

Blair packs our guns and brings extra ammunition on Monday night. She is determined with lofty goals. "I want to pick up a gun, blast, and hit the bull's eye without hesitation." Blair had watched too many Westerns growing up. An Annie Oakley goal is beyond her, but she'll have fun trying. "It is wonderful doing something other than bar hopping or going straight home." She waves to the manager, who drops what he is doing to cater to us.

"Roger, cover for me." Hunter escorts us to the firing range. "I'm glad to see you, gals. It means you are taking gun ownership seriously."

"You have no idea. I want to reach an expert level. Any suggestions for today?"

"Did you practice loading this week?" Hunter tries to hide his amusement.

Blair shows him her clip and proceeds to load the gun, making sure there is no bullet in the chamber.

"Well done." The manager smiles at her dedication and watches me do the same. "Well, Blair, you learned to squeeze last time. Let's see if you can remember how."

We put on our protective glasses and earmuffs. Blair takes a wide stance, lines up the site, and gently pulls back on the trigger, missing the target completely. She moans.

"Something wrong, Blair?"

"I think so. A teen used a gun this week to commit suicide. I guess my subconscious is battling. How could a teen get hold of a gun anyway?"

"First of all, guns don't kill. People do. If they didn't have guns to commit suicide, they'd hang themselves or stick their head in a gas stove. So, don't make the gun your enemy."

"Yes, but a teen, Hunter, still a little boy?"

"You brought up a hot topic. Bear with me for a minute. Our store sold you a gun. You filled out forms and waited two days for our background check before you took the gun home. If a teen under eighteen comes in, we turn them away.

"But if that same kid goes to a private gun show, he can walk out with anything he wants—no wait time either. A young person with an assault weapon probably got it from there or stole it. I, for one, disagree that a kid should be able to buy any gun anywhere. Hell, their brains continue to grow until they are twenty-five, with all their hormones raging, too. Retailers and private sellers should come up with a conscience-oriented sales system. The two-day wait period is too easy. For assault weapons, it should be months of waiting with thorough background checks that include mental health testing.

"But I'm only the manager here. My boss disagrees with me and doesn't want me to discuss it with customers. Fortunately, you've learned how a lack of concentration can affect your shooting. Try to let the emotions go and concentrate on the target." He keeps his voice level and calm during his explanation.

"Thank you for that, Hunter. I hadn't realized any of that information. You answered my concerns, so now let me try again. Blair takes a deep breath and squeezes the trigger on the exhale, nailing the target between the eyes.

"Excellent! Clearing your head of emotion works every time."

Hunter continues to give pointers to both of us, and we decide to practice on Mondays and Wednesdays. Of course, just the two of us attending isn't good enough for Blair. She is determined to get her friends involved, too.

I imagine heated viewpoints flying during the next GNO.

Chapter 10

This week, Debbie suggests a less crowded venue. We meet in a new restaurant on the bayside of Amelia, where the St. Mary's River winds past downtown. We mosey along on cobblestoned Centre Street, managing to find parking nearby.

The Pelican, one of the renovated warehouse buildings, sits by the railroad tracks. You can see the marina from the second floor and watch a diverse group of boaters fuel up. Some are local shrimpers and charter fishing boats. Large yachts dock, too, for the pleasure of sightseeing in our quaint town of Fernandina Beach, the birthplace of the shrimping industry.

The town also boasts the first railway station in Florida and the first bar, The Palace Saloon. This local favorite resembles a western-movie saloon with tin ceilings and a long mahogany bar.

The Pelican is up and coming and, thankfully, quieter than the saloon.

Debbie texts us: "I'm here. Holding a table for y'all."

I bet she's drinking already.

"Are we early, or are the other two late?" Blair asks when we find her table.

"Neither. Sam and Meghan are traveling from Jax. They should be here soon."

"What are you drinking?"

"Madras. I'm tired of wine and sweet island drinks. A little cranberry juice with vodka is my favorite in the evenings."

"Okay, I'll have something too…maybe a Pina colada? It certainly suits the décor," Blair laughs. "And tourist drinks aren't strong—I need to cut back." She pulls back her chair, tipping the artificial palm tree with plastic coconuts. I catch it before it falls to the floor as a server arrives in a straw hat, jeans, and a tee shirt with a huge pelican head on the front.

"I'll have another Madras. Blair will have a Pina colada. Little Sis, still drinking cranberry juice?"

"Yes, I'll switch to Evian later."

"Yes, ma'am." The young server scurries off.

"Debbie, please help me. You know how the girls will react when I talk about the shooting range."

"You bet I know. Our friends hate guns." Debbie smiles mischievously.

"If you are talking about me, it better be good." Sam grabs a stool next to me.

Meghan takes the last seat. "Sorry, we are late. I-95 was a bitch today. How long have crews been working on State Road 200 onto the island? They started it two years ago, didn't they, Debbie?"

"They did. That should be our next mission. I deal with one-lane traffic to and from work every day. I've replaced my tires twice because of it. Now I hear they are fixing on and off-ramps to I-95 before they finish our job. It irritates me to no end that I can't do a thing about it."

"Aiya. I take the back way. Amelia has two bridges, you know. Slower, but prettier and no construction, Megs."

"Good idea. I'll do that next week." Meghan types a reminder into her phone.

"Talking about good ideas, Little Sis and I began shooting lessons last week. We thought you could join us off the island near Yulee on Monday evening."

Meghan holds her hands up, shaking her head. "Seriously? You know I hate guns. They scare me, and I refuse to hold one."

"Would you rather someone else held one against you?" Debbie asks sharply.

"Of course not. That is a silly question, and you know it."

"Then I suggest you overcome the fear, darlin', and spend a few hours a week learning how to handle one for nothing more than defensive use if the need ever arises like Blair and Char are doing."

"Aiya. I understand how Meghan feels, but would we be safe without protection if the economy falls into the toilet again? Walking a bag of groceries into our homes could be dangerous. When the grocery stores run out of food, things will be more pearlyous."

"Pearlyous?" Debbie asks.

"Maybe you mean perilous?" Meghan asks.

"Okay. Unsafe." Sam rationalizes with her general perspective of a world economic collapse and a looming grey cloud that follows overhead. "Guns·scare me, but I try it at the shooting range. Okay, Char and Blair, you can count me in on Monday night."

Debbie says, "I know how to shoot, but I could practice. I'll think about it."

Meghan shifts in her seat. "No fair, girlfriends, y'all are pushing me into a corner. Okay, I will try it once. Just once!"

"And I'll swing by to pick you up in case you forget about it." Sam gives Meghan a brief hug and a giggle.

"Forget about it? I am going to dread it for the next four days."

"I say we toast; here's to overcoming our fears." Sam cheers everyone on.

"Here, here—overcoming our fears," Deb and Blair echo while a reluctant Meghan lifts her glass. I play along.

"So, Meghan, we hear you attached yourself to that sweetheart, William, the public defender?" Debbie teases. "How serious is it?"

"More like he attached himself to me. I don't know. Will's a kind man and smart, but it's only been a week."

"Well, does he make you, you know, happy?" Debbie winks at Sam.

"You know I don't like talking about sexual things." Meghan blushes.

"Yes, I know, that's why I ask." Debbie slyly smiles.

"He was with you when Char and I called early Sunday. I saw him in the background."

"Just because he spent the night doesn't mean we had sex. Let's say he's a good kisser and has my attention for something more…maybe."

"A good kisser! Why are so few guys good at kissing?" Blair wonders aloud.

"They are in a hurry to slide to the lower lips," Debbie explains matter-of-factly.

"Good Lord." Meghan blushes again.

"Really? You always have the most fun. I find that guys who can't smooch more than a few seconds are usually…Blair peeks around and whispers, "Quick-shots. Kissing arouses them too much, and they finish before I'm even warmed up."

Deb smiles. "I know what a quick shot is."

"Oh? You've had them, too?"

"No, I never had one, but I understand the terminology." Debbie gulps her Madras.

"I can't be the only one here that experienced men who can't control their orgasm?"

The girls glance at each other and shrug.

Sam laughs. "Aiya. You are the weakest link in this chain."

"So, what is it that attracts that kind to me? Why me?" Blair worries.

Sam pats her hand. "Don't worry. Maybe you are so pretty; they are halfway there when you say yes to a date?"

"Well, that is nice of you to say. But maybe they want to get it over with and leave?" Blair hangs her head.

"Do they do that? Have sex with you and then scurry away?" Debbie asks, looking upset for her friend.

"No. Now that I think about it, it's usually the quick ones who are ready to marry me, but I'm pushing them out the door."

An intense look flashes on my sister's face.

"Hello, Blair—Earth to Blair." Sam tries not to laugh. "It's nothing to be ashamed of."

"No. I thought about Seth and Trish that night at Yoga and how Seth hurt his mother and pushed her out the door. Debbie, remember what we saw at the funeral?"

"Hm."

"Aiya. What does 'hm' mean? What did you two see?"

Debbie answers. "Her husband demonstrated the

same elbow action the kid did to his mom at the yoga class. She winced in pain at the funeral, too."

Meghan raises her eyebrows. "That behavior might be worth getting on video and handing it to the correct officials. Trish sounds like a battered wife and mom."

"I'll have Jack's girlfriend slash secretary investigate it. She's my new P.I. Jack said she flunked out of the FBI program and has had a boulder on her shoulder ever since. She would be eager to find out who killed him for sure. I'd hate to be on her enemy list."

"Will she be discreet with the information, Deb?" Blair seems irritated.

I don't like the idea of someone else spying around, either.

Debbie snickers. "Do you think I'm a stooge? She's good for our needs. Hey, if she goes crazy and finds out it was Seth who started the fire that killed her boyfriend, his death should give her some peace, and it will save us a lot of work. We can move on to someone or something else needing our attention."

"Maybe it's time for your P.I. to follow Daddy dearest," Blair says.

"He has a thriving OB/GYN practice." Meghan shakes her head. "That means showing up for regular hours and anytime a patient is about to give birth."

"It takes time and planning to be a killer," Sam says. "Besides, people who bring babies into the world won't be killing them, will they?"

"It does sound weird," Meghan says.

"He's an OB/GYN, but two of his babies died? That is weirder still," Blair says.

"So, let's guess it isn't Daddy dearest. We've been treating Trish as a victim, but what if we label her a

murderer and then figure out why she would do it?"
Debbie suggests.

"Why would she do what? Kill her babies? Kill
Seth? A puppy? Set a house on fire and kill two people
in it?" Meghan thinks deeply. "No. Someone is covering
for someone."

"Let's order food. I've been waking up hungover
and starved on Friday mornings. Maybe a little food
might help."

"Blair, the lightweight. We're drinking two to your
one, but you get hungover. Could we have some menus,
please?" Sam finds Blair's inability to hold liquor
laughable.

"I know; I'm a wimp, but I'm trying my best. Oh,
the club sandwich looks great."

I sit smugly after my order—no sense interrupting
their train of thought. Besides, if the doctor or the mother
is as guilty as Seth, they should face the consequences.

Chapter 11

Blair and I meet Meghan and Sam at the shooting range. Sam is anxious. Her voice registers higher than usual while Meghan stands stiff as a board, refusing to look us in the eyes.

Hunter brings weapons and headphones for the newcomers. Debbie opted out because she is working on lesson plans for a new course that she wants to teach on emotional intelligence.

"Okay, ladies. I hear you're uncomfortable with guns. That's good because it tells me you respect the damage they can do."

While Blair and I practice shooting, Hunter teaches Meghan and Sam how to hold and load the gun. Then, they move to target practice. I stop to watch Hunter place the weapon in Meghan's hand.

"Ugh." She cringes as though it is covered in a communicable disease.

"You are using it for defensive purposes only. For now, though, get used to the feel of a weapon in your hands without the clip—no bullets. I'll have Sam step up to shoot first."

Seth's depraved actions affected Sam more than anyone realized—anyone but me. I feel a kindred spirit in Sam. Maybe I could share my inner self with her one day. We both have deep-seated passions, but I hold more conviction than she does. Still, we could make a great team going after the bad guys and standing up for what is right.

As Hunter pulls the target closer, I remove my headphones. I want to hear and see as Sam squeezes the trigger. Her first shot misses. "Sam, like I tell everyone, it helps to keep your eyes open. Line up the site."

Sam tries again but misses. I motion to get her attention. She gives the gun to Hunter and lifts her headset.

"Sam, pretend it's a poacher who would think nothing of harming an innocent puppy or an elephant."

We connect; she nods, and her concentration increases as my words sink in, giving her something she can relate to.

"One more try." Sam positions her headgear. She takes a deep breath and shoots.

"Wow. You got him right in the heart. I don't know if that's beginner's luck or what, but go ahead and take a few more shots. Remember to squeeze the trigger, not pull."

Sam holds her focus and her anger. The poacher suffers bullets to the stomach and another right through his face. She snickers. "That'll teach the bastard."

I give Sam a thumbs up. Meghan is next, and she doesn't look happy. Blair notices and takes a break.

"Okay, Meghan, it's your turn, but don't feel pressured by Sam's performance. Let's insert the clip. Now, I want you to concentrate on holding the gun in a proper stance." Meghan stands the way Hunter positions her. "Don't worry about hitting the target the first time out. Just learn to squeeze the trigger."

Meghan nods as a bead of sweat rolls down from her eye. "If Sam can do this, I can do this; I refuse to be the group's wuss." She takes another deep breath. " …keep my eyes open." She speaks aloud, remembering the instructions Hunter had given to Sam. "Line up my site."

Sam sighs. "Do it, Meg, pull the trigger…sometime today."

The color drains from Meghan's face as the gun blasts.

"Right through the heart, Meghan. Right through the heart," Hunter roars, genuinely surprised and happy for his terrified student.

"Way to go, Megs. You did it. You did it," Blair cheers.

"Yes, I did, but I could use some water." Her face pales to marshmallow white.

"That was a big step for you. You gals are something else. Will I see you again?"

"Of course, Hunter. I had fun." Sam studies him up and down.

"Meghan, how about it?" Hunter asks.

She takes a long swig of her bottled water. "I did it once. I can do it again—maybe even two shots next time."

****

"She what? Are you serious?" Debbie nibbles on her evening snack during the Skype session. "I would have lost that bet. I thought Meghan would have bolted out the door."

"Me too." Blair laughs. "And Sam annihilated her target once she treated it as a poacher." Blair smiles at the computer screen. "It's nice being together again. We were always simpatico, you know? Having you back in our lives did the trick. You always were the instigator, keeping us on our toes."

"Yes, that's me, little Miss Mastermind. But remember to give yourself kudos for this one. Okay, dinner's ready, doll. Later." Deb clicks off Skype.

Blair beams. She says hanging out with her friends was like being in college—lots of laughs and camaraderie but without all the study hours.

"How can Debbie eat dinner at this time of night and not gain weight? That girl has it all." Blair takes her glass of nonfat milk to her room and turns on The Phantom of the Opera, hoping to sleep. The same music agitates my brain.

My phone sounds a notification—a text from Sam.

—*Still awake?*—

—*Hard to sleep listening to Blair's Broadway ballads.*—

—*LOL. Blair loves those ballads still? She didn't buy earbuds yet? Poor you.*—

—*You know Blair—not worth the effort to convert her.*—

—*I hear you. She won't understand why you don't like her music. I went through that with her.*—

—*Not to depress or irritate you, but I'm sending links that will keep us both more aware of animal rights, and if you want, you can join me in signing petitions. Check it out. Maybe we can do something about animal abuse together.*—

—*I'll look at them in the morning. I want a peaceful sleep.*—

—*Aiya. Sorry, I'll remember to send bad news in the morning next time.*—

—*No worries, Sam. I'm glad we're on the same team. Oh, and Sam?*—

—*Yeah?*—

—Your shooting impressed me. Goodnight.—
—Thanks. Night, Char.—

I don't like long conversations, so I cut Sam off. But I open the links immediately. They include petition sites to protect whales and dolphins from military sonar testing. Links for animals treated viciously in Thailand, Africa, American circuses, and others to enact laws against skinning animals while alive.

Another article talks about African poachers using military precision to kill elephant families for their tusks, which the Far East population demands. Baby elephants don't have any horns. A mother protected her baby and took on the bullets, but they killed the baby anyway. My anger is growing exponentially. Poachers need consequences. I want to shut them down but am not litigious like Meghan. I'm not vocal or social like Sam.

But I am physically active, robust, and intellectually more capable than I let on. I want to be close to majestic creatures while safeguarding them. A plan formulates in my mind. Before my eyes close, I complete a basic strategy for my future and the animals that need me.

Then, I dream of poachers.

I show them no mercy as they fall one by one by my hand.

Chapter 12

"Okay, ladies. The P.I. is on the job," Debbie announces after we arrive for GNO and settle into the first drink. "She helped find the connection between Seth and the fire that killed Jack."

"What? How?" I can't believe Meghan is surprised.

"The fire inspector deemed it arson but couldn't find anything as evidence on the property."

"That's right, but while workers bulldozed Mr. Allen's house, they took down a tree hollowed out by either a lightning strike or old age.

"Anyway, my P.I. sees a piece of red sticking out from the remaining stump. She pulls a container out and a pair of black leather gloves from under it. Long story short, Seth's DNA is all over the gloves. Authorities are testing the type of accelerant as we speak. But, ladies, it's official. Seth started the fire."

"Well, I am glad that one mystery is solved," Meghan says dryly.

Debbie continues. "Step one finished. Seth's guilt is driving the P.I. to complete the job."

"Doing what?" Meghan asks.

"Finding Seth's killer, of course."

"Aiya. He shot himself. Why bother to stir the pot? I'm glad he's dead, I wish I killed the turd." Sam throws back another shot of tequila. "He knew he couldn't get away with the fire. Ha! He was right."

We look at each other, baffled. The comment wasn't something that would come out of Sam's mouth so early in the evening, but she is drinking tequila and started before us.

"You just learned to shoot. Now, you say you could murder someone?" Blair asks.

"I'm not talking about just anyone. Besides, who says I would use a gun? A knife is effective, too." Sam gestures with her finger, slicing her throat.

"Have a problem you want to talk about?" Meghan eyes her friend.

"Yes. I'm angry." Sam's face reddens, and her eyes glare painfully.

"You've been cross-posting animals and horrible news about them again?"

Sam crosses her arms and nods.

Meghan continues gently. "Sharing bad news with other animal advocates is depressing. Maybe you need to take a vacation from it for a while."

Everyone squeezes in appetizers and requests a new round as Sam takes a deep breath and continues. "I'm happy for elephant reserves like the one in Tennessee that rescues performing elephants. They live there free for the rest of their lives. I'm sorry, but I'm pertur-be-ded. No one is doing enough to prevent animal abuse and killing. How can I help change that?"

Debbie answers, "Sam, darling, it's perturbed. And you are helping; you are an advocate. You tell me things that I didn't know were going on. Listen, it boils down to laws and their enforcement. I don't know the regulations in Africa or anywhere else in the world, but to start with, we can work on policies here to protect these beautiful creatures and all animals.

"Humanity must evolve if animals are to survive and be treasured," Meghan says while patting Sam's hand. "We all agree that you opened our eyes to the atrocities we are sometimes too busy, too shallow, or too appalled to understand thoroughly." Her words soothe Sam, who takes a deep breath and lets it out.

My poker face fails me as I fight back rage for Sam's pain and the animals she loves. Sam notices my anger.

"I'm sorry, Char. Meghan's right. I need to stop cross-posting for a while."

"Don't apologize—I'm glad for the awareness, no matter how painful. I want to help, too."

Sam squeezes my arm. I often feel her studying me, wondering which way I roll—lesbian or bi, like her. She knows me on a deeper level, somehow. Her eyes empathize with me and convey that she feels sorry for how Blair patronizes me.

Yes, my sister helps me through college and puts a roof over my head, but a close emotional family bond is absent. Sam doesn't understand that I'm comfortable with our lack of sisterhood. Unlike Blair, confrontation excites me, while my sister creates a haven of denial. For the first time, the women of GNO become quiet simultaneously, each drawn into a silent daydream.

"Ladies, how about another round?" The server places a bowl of snacks on the table.

"Sure. Bring another round and give me the tab," Deb says.

Tonight, a seed drops into fertile soil and takes root. Regena told me I would come to no good. But tonight, I commit to twisting her opinion into a positive intention for change. I will implement my plan, becoming a gardener, choking out putrid weeds for the animals and

Sam.

Finally, my life has direction and purpose; I find my passion. I will study everything about South Africa and the species I want to protect there. The extinction of elephants and rhinos is unacceptable; I will save them by studying survival techniques and committing geography to memory. I will learn what plants contain water and the trees that provide fruit. I will study those tribes and dialects that can help me. I will become a predator, learning to track my prey, the poachers.

Unable to divulge my plans, I must fool Blair by doubling my class load and graduating early. That will allow me plenty of time to ready myself, perfect my lofty ideas, and turn them into a workable reality.

I sock the pillow a few times tonight, laying my head on it with a wave of serenity I had never felt before. Taking care of creation moves me and gives me direction and a purpose.

****

I'm happy it's Monday; we all meet at the shooting range. Our focus and dedication impress Hunter. I study how his gentleness affects Meghan. He takes her as far as her psyche allows her to go but presses no further. Although she hates violence, he finesses her to the point where she can use a gun spontaneously if she must.

Hunter sees a tremendous improvement in my usually reserved manner. "What's changed in you, Char? Your shooting was always good, but now it is incredible."

I point to my head. He nods, understanding what I mean. Attitude is everything.

Although Blair wants to be a perfect shot, she isn't me. She bristles at my target, which is filled with bull's eyes. She tries hard to compete with me, not understanding why I should be better at everything.

Big Sister's scowl drilled holes through me while I was growing up. They don't anymore. She has no idea what more I can do. I won't stand in the shadows forever.

Months pass, and I exceed my expectations at the range. I learn how to shoot a rifle and graduate to other, more complicated weapons. Hunter encourages me to enter competitions, but I decline. "I shoot for enjoyment only." He suspects something about me but can't figure it out.

****

For my college graduation present, Blair offers an extended trip to a destination of my choice.

"South Africa, thank you."

For two years, I've spent every waking moment narrowing information down to South Africa's geography, politics, and diverse network of languages. I learned dialects of indigenous tribes who might cooperate with my quest. I learned the migratory habits of each species—what they eat and who eats them. I'm armed with the knowledge to survive and thrive while stopping poachers.

Some people hear a calling to be Seals, the elite branch of the military that puts their lives on the line every minute. My purpose is the same caliber: safeguarding endangered species. I will be a mercenary to save their lives and give them a future.

****

"Well, if this isn't a switch-a-roo. I'm getting you up in the morning? Come on, Little Sis, it's Saturday. We need to shop for your safari."

I sit up, shocked. "I stayed up the night reviewing

our trip. Sorry. Yes, I'll need good boots, mosquito netting, lots of bug spray…."

"Don't forget dresses for nightlife, too. But let's start with coffee first, shall we?"

Dresses? Okay. I'll agree, for now. The time nears when I must confiscate a couple of Blair's high-limit charge cards to arrange a purchase of rifles and ammo and have them waiting for me once I'm on the continent.

Shopping will be an opportune time to watch and learn as she uses her credit card numbers and codes. Sometimes, you must break a rule to do something more significant than honesty and integrity guidelines dictate. Blair won't know I used her cards until she receives the bills. Those statements will arrive a month after I use them—timing is everything. My passport finally arrives one week before departure.

GNO will continue with Meghan presenting an outline for new laws that she has already submitted in our state of Florida—regulations that would severely punish animal abusers.

Other work includes educational recommendations to institute emotional intelligence classes from preschool through high school. The mandatory courses would teach love and compassion for all living things to the poorest of our society. They would also note the children who felt nothing or, worse, felt pleasure kicking a puppy or sitting on a kitty.

Would early intervention change the course of a sociopath's life? Or would ostracizing them protect the general population as they got older? Would preschool children viewed as sociopaths have a place in society, or could they be cured? Or would they be institutionalized and never see freedom?

The ladies have been working on rulings for years. It would take more time to pass laws and for new generations to benefit from them. But I won't wait. Animals can't hold on much longer. Who knows how many species Kony and other warlords will destroy?

Alias Fund Me pages create substantial bank accounts waiting for me in South Africa. I've researched black markets to manufacture passports for each account; I cannot risk detection. I must have cash to buy weapons and supplies continually and to pay my guides until I no longer need them.

Mother was wrong about me being a freak. Instead, I am a savior in the making—a redeemer of helpless animals. At every chance, I increase my preparedness. Before bed, I place another weight on the bar and lift two hundred pounds—not good enough. I will do better. Weaklings don't survive in the jungle.

****

Once we arrive at the airport, Blair begins to preach. "Sam, I'm trusting you with Little Sis's life. You know that, don't you?"

"Wrong, Blair. Sam is responsible for Sam. I'm responsible for myself. You should understand that principle at your age."

"I…well…okay then, Little Sis."

As usual, Blair retreats from confrontation. If she only knew me, my sister wouldn't worry.

"You do have your passport?"

"Yes, of course." I wave it in Blair's face. *I won't ever see her again, anyway.*

"You took a beautiful photo; I didn't know you could apply makeup. People will mistake you for a model." She laughs nervously. "The dress is becoming on you, too. Doesn't she look gorgeous, ladies?"

They all agree, but they don't understand. I planned to appear stunning for my photo and flight to Africa. Once there, I won't resemble anything like my passport photo. I give the ladies an obligatory hug before I walk to my gate, away from their access.

Sam hesitates, lagging to hug her friends. Their concern about me is understandable. I overheard their conversations the night before as Sam championed my cause.

"Char needs this trip. She'll come back more relaxed than ever, Blair. You wait and see."

"I hope so. She's turned defiant this past year. I hope you can handle her."

"Aiya. I don't handle Char. I let her be who she wants to be. It is her life, after all, not yours."

"Yes, I know, but steer her in the right direction, promise?"

"Promise," Sam said half-heartedly, knowing Blair would never understand.

My nerves feel overstimulated, too excited; I'm so close to my quest but not there yet. I need something to calm me. "Give me a whiskey," I order at a bar near my gate. Along with deep breathing, it is enough to help refocus my deception before my first flight.

"You with a real drink? You worried about the flight, Char?" Sam asks as she sits next to me.

"No, not worried—excited. The alcohol will act as a sleep medication on the way over. I want to be ready to move as soon as we arrive at our destination."

"Smart. You'll love nighttime flights. I sleep during long, boring plane trips to anywhere."

****

I'm glad that I listened to her wisdom. We awake refreshed and ready to go. She smiles, proud of herself.

"Well, how about that, Char? No cramped legs, no boredom, and a smooth flight. Soon, we will land and begin our holiday."

Fifteen minutes later, the pilot makes an announcement. "Ladies and gentlemen, we're having trouble with our landing gear. No worries; we have protocols to follow for this situation. But we may circle for some time. Please remain seated with fastened seat belts as stormy weather is rolling our way. I expect a bumpy ride until we land."

Sam is standing and stretching happily when the announcement comes over the speaker. Her mood turns.

"Aiya. I'm calling the airline about this. Maybe we get some money back because I don't pay for landing gear trouble."

As she utters "trouble," the plane jumps up and down. Instinctively, I grab Sam as she propels out of our row. I pull her toward me, enveloping her on my lap as the plane veers left and right and suddenly dives. Baggage compartments open and close. People scream frantically.

Impossible. My life can't end before I begin my purpose. During a moment of stability, I help Sam sit and yank on her seatbelt, tightening it.

The pilot announces, "Sorry about that, folks. Again, remain seated and buckled. We're through the worst of the weather. On a happier note, the landing gear is now functional, and we are waiting for our turn to land in the next thirty minutes or so."

I grab a bag out of the seat pocket in front of me and vomit. For the first time, I'm rattled, but I'm not sure why.

"You, okay, Char?"

"I am. The bumpiness upset my stomach."

"I told you to eat something, but you didn't. Anyway, thank you."

"For what?"

"You saved me. You kept me from flying into the aisle, hurting myself."

"Oh, of course."

Is that the reason I'm sick? I recall how I felt when Sam was in danger, and I vomit again.

Chapter 13

Debbie

Poor Blair believes something doesn't feel right about Charlotte. Her stomach began aggravating her once she agreed to the African trip. Suddenly, Char became Miss Independent, possessed with a single-minded goal of seeing a country none of us had considered visiting before.

Sam's the only one not bothered by it. "She's maturing late, finally coming out of her shell. Let her be."

We wait until Sam and Char board the plane, watching it take off safely. I'm jealous of everyone coming and going, as I haven't found time to travel in years. Still, I can't wait to hear about their first week's adventure. I made Sam promise to Skype.

Blair says she doesn't know whether to feel relieved of her responsibility or worry even more about her little sister. Meghan and I had put our heads together, knowing Blair's anxieties might grow after the plane is out of sight.

"Okay, Meghan, it's officially GNO time. Blair is in crisis."

"A glass of wine before we head home sounds good," Meg says.

Blair agrees with a huge sigh.

Meghan pats her hand. "Show a little faith, my friend."

"This may sound awful, but I'm relieved Little Sis is gone. She needed to go somewhere before I booted her out of my house."

"She has changed in the past six months," Meghan agrees. "She has come out of her shell, for sure."

"Out of her mind is more like it. No offense meant Blair, but she's argumentative and darn right bitchy. Where did our Little Sis go, and why?" I grab the empty table next to us. "Let's sit, ladies."

I rarely sit and eat at an airport bar, with everyone rushing to eat, drink, and go. But, Blair seems lost and in shock, like a war veteran with PTSD.

"Maybe I should have insisted on a physical when she got those immunizations for travel. Maybe we exposed her to too much nastiness in the world, as though she didn't get enough of it from Mom. Maybe Little Sis is going through delayed puberty in a sense. Her teenage years were straight from hell—she didn't know how to relate to regular people like us.

"It's like she's experiencing her rebellious stage now instead of at fifteen or so. It's good that she's evolving because she was much too introverted. Don't you think so?" Blair asks, wanting our votes of confidence.

I try to bring up a sticky topic. "Blair, you saw the way Charlotte took to Sam, right? It's like they communicate without even talking. They have an understanding, if you know what I mean?"

My ever-socially-obtuse friend stares right through me. "No, I don't know what you mean, except they react to injustices with too much sensitivity."

I sigh. Blair is brilliant with numbers but clueless with the rest of life. Meghan nods at me and takes over.

"Is there a possibility that Charlotte is gay but doesn't know it yet…or is afraid to come out to you?"

"Gay? Little Sis?" Blair laughs as though the thought is brand new to her. Sadly, I think it is. "Oh, wait. Does that happen to molested girls? Do they go gay? Because I suspect one of Mom's boyfriends got away with that, but Little Sis wouldn't confide in me."

Meghan gently says, "I don't know, Blair, that's something you might want to research. Debbie and I think it is a possibility, and the sooner you accept that prospect, maybe the tension will ease up between you and Little Sis, I mean Charlotte. We should stop calling her Little Sis; she is twenty-one."

"But that's her nickname; she's used to it."

I hope to make a dent in Blair's armor of denial. "Only because you haven't given her a choice between anything else. Engage the brain, please, my dear friend."

"That's a mean phrase. Please stop saying it. But you think I may be causing her to act out? I see what you mean. I've always worried she would blame me for escaping our house without her. Maybe my offer to take her in should have come much sooner. Do you think she hates me for that?"

Compassionate Meghan reaches across the table. "What is done is done. You are here for her now and have been for three years. She has learned what a normal household feels like…well, semi-normal anyway."

Blair handles the joke well. To her credit, she knows where she comes from and never pretends otherwise. She told us that remembering her childhood spurs her on to do better. I hide what I think: the memories that encourage Blair affect her sister negatively.

Something about Char's darkness concerns me; she built a quiet wall around herself, defending it like a knight in armor. Too many times, I pushed my concerns away. After all, I wasn't the mommy type. I didn't want her to attach to me as she had with Sam, who enjoys mentoring the girl.

"She has never been out of the country, has she?"

"No. She never had a passport, although I wanted to expose her to other cultures but never could take enough time off work. Okay, the truth is, I forgot about it after a while. What's that saying… the road to hell is paved with good intentions?"

"No, I do not believe that. You are a good-hearted soul, but we all get caught up in life, our jobs, school, and love. The Creator also judges by our good intentions, and yours were right."

I bristle. "Whoa, lost me there, Meghan. Don't start the God stuff with me, judgment, tribulations…"

"I am talking about love, Debbie. That is what our higher power is—pure love."

I am about to go into my usual atheistic comments, but Meghan gives me a wink and shakes her head. She meant those words for fragile Blair, not me—no need to engage in that topic.

Blair speaks in a drone. "Char better treat Sam well, behave around her, and not act like a brat. Sam hasn't vacationed in years and needs a good time on this trip as she gathers information about animal abuse policies there."

I order wine for the table, doubting one drink will fix Blair's worry. "If you ask me, I just said goodbye to two ladies who will have a better time over there while we stay home and work our butts off. Stop worrying."

I have enough of Blair's whining. "Let's peek at the menu, ladies. We may as well eat."

"Really? I'm craving some fried shrimp."

As always, food seems like a good distraction for my friend. At least it takes her mind off Charlotte. Meghan nods at my ulterior motive. The three of us sit around the table, agreeing to keep GNO going while Sam and Char are away.

Also, I insist we continue Saturday night out, although Meghan has found William. Now, it is Blair's turn to find a special someone because the right relationship would balance her life. She should explore the non-numerical side of herself. Let's face it: she needs to make love regularly with someone who will adore her.

I hope Cupid will grace her with his appearance on Saturday night.

****

After a long day of teaching, kicking off my shoes and placing my aching feet on my cool marble floors is a relief. That and a madras inside the valentine gold-rimmed glass Gregory gave me begins a beautiful evening.

I love my marsh view when it glistens during high tide. A flock of wood storks fly by, only to turn around mid-flight to land in the marsh before me.

"Don't you dare," I laugh. Pregnancy isn't on my agenda.

A roseate spoonbill wades in the shallows, unbothered by the storks settling all around. If another roseate lands, it would be lovely. *I'm trying to be a cupid to wildlife, but I haven't tested my abilities yet on Blair.* Poor Blair. My matchmaking skills better be sharp because I'm determined to find her a proper beau. Why haven't I thought of this earlier?"

My cousin's face flashes in my mind. Albert Finney and I are third cousins; I've known him since we were tots, but his family lacks the money that mine has because they are all artists. Albert's mother, my Aunt Lucretia, was a singer in his father's jazz band. Some say her silky yet soul-shaking voice could have made it big in the business.

When Albert was born, Lucretia gave up nightclub life. She said that once she saw her baby, she knew her path in life would be nurturing the son who had stolen her heart. She could think of nothing else.

Early on, both parents knew Albert would follow an artist's path, and their son proved them right. He makes a decent living with his paintings and sculptures, finally rising to a position of renown. But my cousin cares little about fame and fortune. He wants only to glorify what he calls "creation." I don't mean he is a religious fanatic; instead, he's more generic, more spiritual. Albert connects with the unseen, like abstract angels and ethereal lights too silly for my heathen tastes. But the public can't seem to get enough.

Maybe my cousin is what a doctor would prescribe for Blair's loneliness. Plus, Albert is eye candy—plain and simple. It isn't that he has a big-screen or magazine-cover handsomeness. Instead, he has the structural correctness that a photographer craves. His elongated face bears a masculine nose—strong and perfectly proportioned. His lips, to me, are his sexiest attribute—all-male but available in a sexy way. He stands about six feet tall with a rugged body. Yep, Blair's type.

Behind his lips is a smile everyone loves to see;

Albert's grin lights up a room. His bright green eyes search and study, but not in a cruel way—not at all judgmental. They are soulful but, most of all, kind. I'd like to see more anger in his work, but admirers feel comforted by his mellowness.

It never occurred to me earlier to pair Albert with Blair. After all, I only see him on family holidays and special occasions. That's what is so strange about the pairing—my slightly neurotic Blair matched with Albert, steady-going and unhurried.

I call her. "Hey, why don't you join Greg and me on Saturday at the gallery? They are exhibiting my cousin's work."

"You won't mind a third wheel? Hey, since when do you have a cousin who is an artist?"

"You don't know Albert? Hm. I mentioned him over the years, I'm sure."

"You didn't, but I'd still like to go, thanks."

"What are you thinking about, sweetie?" Greg pours a glass of wine and joins me on the couch. My fiancé laughs when I share my matchmaking plans.

"Okay, I'll go along with your little game. But if Blair and Albert don't click, you keep the night going with some clever banter while I sit back and enjoy the crash scene."

"Hmm. Do you think failure is on my agenda?"

"No, honey; I've learned to expect anything and everything when I'm with you. I've edited so much today; I need a good outing. Your attempt at playing Cupid could provide a much-needed distraction. Hmm, that's a thought. Keep your cupid costume for the bedroom." Greg chuckles.

I cozy up to him. "And what if they click? Will your

entertainment be ruined for the night?"

"No, sweetheart. I will never run out of enjoyment living with you, and I wouldn't have it any other way."

Gregory loves to pull me close by pressing his hands on my derriere. His lips are tender, searching, and passionate. When we kiss, we melt together. He opens his eyes and nods toward the stairs. He doesn't need to convince me.

Wiggling out of his grip, I begin to peel off my clothes piece by piece as I slowly climb the staircase. Gregory watches until I reach the top. I throw my panties over my shoulder and vanish. Our clothes lay from the living room to the bedroom when he reaches me.

He struts with anticipation. This man, without a doubt, loves me for me—not for my money and not just for sex. Well, sure, it's about sex, but that's on both of our agendas. I can't love anyone more than I love Greg. *Oh, my, an epiphany!*

Without any fear of losing my independence, I realize Greg is the one … the man who will be my life partner. I push him onto the mattress and begin to explore every inch of his body with my lips, spurred on by his moans of pleasure.

Chapter 14

Greg and I meet Blair at the gallery at three o'clock. Supporters of the arts expanded the building through the years. The outside walls display the locals' mosaic handiwork, which includes shapes like flying dragons, iguanas, and whimsical meanderings.

Finally, Greg spots Blair. "Did we keep you waiting, girlfriend?"

"No, I just got here; I haven't stepped inside yet—just peeking through the window. Already, I can tell I'm going to love this artist, and you know I'm fussy."

Blair gives us each a quick embrace. That's a strange comment from someone who rarely activates her right brain, but I give Greg a nudge so he notes that things are already leaning in the right direction.

"Did I tell you the artist is my cousin, Albert?"

"Yes, but since when do you have a cousin on Amelia?"

"I didn't. Albert lived in St. Augustine but moved here recently."

"Well, that's Amelia's luck. It looks like they're going to set up outside, too. Are we early?"

"Just a bit. I'd like to see Albert before he gets too busy. Since I consider you family, you get to meet my artsy relations. But I don't see him anywhere."

This is one time I'm glad for Blair's naivety. Mesmerized by the paintings, she is clueless about my agenda.

"Stop poking me, sweetheart."

Greg understands that my plan is working so far.

Amelia Island's Art gallery opened its extension for Albert's show. It isn't a big room inside, but the canvas-covered patio will hold most of his work. As we open the door, a group of volunteers carry out and hang the pieces that will welcome guests. As the last painting floats by, Greg is sweating, and Blair fans herself with her program. A slight breeze from the Intracoastal waterway provides some relief. Still, my two loves sigh happily as they step into the chill of air conditioning.

When Albert sees me, he saunters over, wrapping his strength around me. I don't understand how someone who paints can be physically strong, too, as though he were a weightlifter. But that is Albert—unique in every way.

Greg and Albert shake hands while Blair stares at a painting just inside the door.

"Ah, Blair, would you like to meet Albert?"

"Your cousin, the genius? Of course, I would, but look at this composition. I can't take my eyes off it; the colors blend seamlessly." She giggles. "There's an angelic being windsurfing with others in what looks to be the Caribbean Sea. Maybe the angel is there to protect people but decides to have some fun, too? Ha! Look at the dolphins riding the wake that the angel stirs up."

Albert winks at me and steps beside my friend. "Do you paint too, Blair?"

"Oh, I wish. I'm right-brain talentless, but I do appreciate great art." Blair finally stands erect and turns to face Albert.

"That's one of my lighter, amusing pieces. I don't

have many."

I edge in. "This is my dearest friend, Blair. Blair, meet the genius, Albert Finney."

"Oh, you? You are Debbie's cousin?"

"Yes, but I've been called worse."

Blair's face turns crimson as Albert stares back, eyes lock. Relief washes over me; I can't help but smile. After all, I broke a cardinal rule of our friendship by setting her up, but it seems to be working. Greg nudges me, conceding early, I bet. He owes me a back rub and a very long massage.

Meanwhile, whether they know it or not, the new couple becomes embarrassingly smitten.

"Albert…ah Albert, my favorite cousin … why don't you give us a quick, personal tour before the guests arrive?"

He answers while still drinking in my friend. "You've seen my work too many times to count, cousin Debbie. But if you allow me, I'll give Blair a tour."

Albert holds out his arm, and without hesitation, Blair places her hand on it.

"What is this, England…eighteen, nineteen hundred, Gregory?" I whisper.

"There is no time where they are; those two are infatuated, obsessed, utterly smitten. You might win two back-rubs for hitting the bull's eye this time."

"Thank you. I'll take you up on that." I give him a butt pat. Until now, men and Blair had always been touch and go, especially in nightclubs where men are likelier to hunt for someone hot and loose, not straight-backed, shy, and uncomfortable.

Blair doesn't display her attractiveness as I do; she wears little makeup, ignores trends, and dissolves into the background. Yet, she scores a touchdown in personality, values, and intelligence, too. That is my darlin' friend's two-edged sword. Men zero in on that naturalness until they realize how bright she is. Then, they either shy away from the relationship or try to conquer her. Sadly, I've watched it happen over and over.

Greg says that regular men, those looking for more than a one-night stand, like her Renaissance body, petite yet curvy with big eyes and silky hair. 'Her body screams motherhood, durable yet womanly soft.' Those sweet attributes will work for her today.

Albert challenges the media's idea of cover girls. He curses the day a sixties model changed the desirable female image. He calls the sixties icon, Twiggy, "a bag of chicken bones that began the ruinous perception of a woman's true figure."

Blair needs an Albert—a man comfortable in his skin. He doesn't want or need a magazine version of eye candy on his arm to feel like a winner. He has the intelligence and sensitivity to see inside a woman and will only accept someone with whom he feels a link. He is genuine and good as gold, the same way Blair is.

As guests come in, they beeline to meet the acclaimed artist who continues to hold Blair's hand on his arm—everyone there assumes they are a couple. As the festivities begin, the procurator calls Albert to the microphone. My cousin flusters; it looks like he doesn't want to disconnect from Blair.

"Cousin, you've been announced; take yourself to the microphone and start the show... think dollars."

"Later, Blair, okay? Cousin, art isn't about the money."

Albert ambles toward the microphone while I grab Blair.

"So, what do you think, girlfriend?" I whisper.

"What do I think?" She answers breathlessly. "Your cousin is beautiful…I mean, brilliant and deep; that's what I think. He said he'd see me later; what did he mean—after the show?"

"Well, Albert said he wanted to join us for dinner afterward. You don't mind, do you?"

"Mind? Oh, no, I don't mind. I'm tickled and honored."

Gregory laughs. "Don't go overboard, Blair. He puts on his pants the same way I do. You don't want him to get a swollen head."

Blair seems dazed. "A swollen head? Oh, no, people like him don't get swollen heads. He isn't self-obsessed. If you don't mind, I'd like to experience each painting again; they're magnificent."

She leaves, drawn to one piece and then another as my cousin dances verbally with admirers.

"Well, Snacks, Blair's been hit with a love bolt straight out of a clear blue sky; I'm glad Albert likes her too." I love it when Greg calls me by sweet nicknames, especially since *Little Debbie* snack cakes are his favorite.

"So, it's not just wishful thinking, then?"

"No, not a fantasy, sweetheart. This time, the arrow hit home. But it's taken you a while with us, hasn't it?"

There it is. Greg means the L-word. But for the first time, I don't want to run, escaping a commitment to maintain my freedom. And he's proven he loves me for me and not just for my money.

Greg's freshly shaved cheek brushes against mine,

and right there, in public, in the middle of an art show, while my cousin schmoozes with the audience, we kiss a kiss that jolts me and confirms we belong to each other.

I have been single long enough.

Chapter 15

The show's successful turnout pleases the art community, which has come out in full force for Albert. Locals order prints, while galleries and fans from around the country buy his originals—all of them.

Employees handle the business end, so the artist is free to go.

"Good, God, I'm famished. I want a stiff drink and a damn good steak if that's alright with you, Blair."

"This amazing artist needs a steak, Debbie…the best steak in town for the best artist in town."

"Ah, if it's steak, we must go to the club, Albert."

I feel full of myself in a beautiful way; it's my first time playing matchmaker, and I've done a fantastic job. I've never seen Blair like this—full of wonder, awe, and appreciation. Albert slew her pessimism in seconds without even trying. We take one car to the club, and Blair slides halfway over in the back seat. Albert positions himself closer to her. After we reach our table, I ask her to join me in the ladies' room.

"Good, God, Blair, snap out of it already."

"All the years we've known each other, you never mentioned Albert. He's wonderful, so masculine on the outside but gentle and kind. Is he this way all the time?"

"Sure enough. My cousin is as genial as they come, and he's authentic—not a game player. He could care less about money—very down to earth, unaffected by all the compliments. He was that way as a kid, too."

"Thank you for this evening...this afternoon. I'll still be grateful if he isn't interested in someone like me. I will know a man like him exists, and I'm not crazy wishing for it."

"Now, don't you worry one bit about that, and let me pee in peace."

"Oh, right, I have to go, too. You mean, Albert does like me?"

"Stop fishing, Blair. I know he does; you know he does. Just take it slow and easy, my friend."

"Okay. Slow it is, but that won't be easy."

Tonight, life changes for Blair and me. She finds Mr. Right, and I realize I have Mr. Right. As we return to our seats, we run into Meghan and Will, who are still dressed from sailing.

"Megs, sweetie, you look radiant, kissed by the sun."

Her skin glows with a tan, two degrees darker than the last time we saw her. She atypically giggles when she gives us each a hug. I suspect her relationship must have reached an intimate level; Will gave her a ticket to Happy Land.

"Perfect timing. Please join us for dinner."

We order a plate of appetizers for the table—Albert's idea. Meghan raises an eyebrow when she sees Blair and Albert sharing their forks.

"Blair, you've got to taste this crab cake," Albert holds his fork to her mouth.

"Mmm. That is good, but the shrimp is tasty, too." She lifts one by the tail and shares. They forget the rest of us who are enjoying seeing love in bloom. I give Megs a discreet thumbs-up, and she mouths, 'Wow.' We are witnessing a side of Blair that we have never seen before.

When the main course arrives, Albert tears through the steak, but Blair hardly touches her food.

"It is delicious, but I ate too many appetizers. I'm not hungry, as usual. Albert, will you share mine?"

Blair had eaten one shrimp and a quarter of a crab cake. Love is a terrific appetite suppressant.

We turn down dessert but order a round of drinks.

"Hey, if y'all don't mind, Blair and I want to stroll on the beach. We'll find a way home afterward. I appreciate the meal," Albert says while escorting my smiling friend outside.

"Did I just witness a miracle?" Meghan asks me.

"We can only hope. But I think so."

"Let me know. Will and I are wiped out and heading straight home."

"We appreciate the food and company. Maybe we can do this again sometime," Will says quickly.

I guess the reason why they want to split. Love is in the air for everyone.

****

Greg and I have a nightcap together when we arrive home.

"What I wouldn't give to have slipped a surveillance camera into Blair's pocket—and Meghan's."

Greg laughs. "Sweetheart, you did your part. I'm sure you will hear from both gals tomorrow."

"Not Meghan—she treasures her privacy. But I expect Blair's call first thing in the morning. She'll reveal the intimate details of her evening with Albert."

"Until then, why don't we make Deb and Greg news?"

"You are insatiable." I meld my body to his.

"Yes, and that's one of the many things you adore about me."

Gregory squeezes me and plants a long, passionate kiss. No other man can arouse me with one kiss as he does. If I choose to one day, I'll have something to tell everyone about our night. But for now, Greg is all mine.

****

This morning, Blair surprises me with nothing; she doesn't call, text, or Skype. I impatiently wait for her to check in all day as I grade papers and sip wine. After five o'clock, she graced me with news.

First, she tells me about Sam and Charlotte. Their flight had arrived safely, and they are enjoying the sites, etc.

"I'm glad to know that, but I'd rather hear about your night with Albert. I've waited all day, you know."

"I'm sorry, Deb, but it was so magical that I held on to it, not wanting to lose its energy."

I can relate to that. "So?"

"We walked barefoot on the beach for hours. We talked a lot, but I can't remember what we said," Blair laughs. "We spotted shooting stars, splashed each other with sparkly phosphorus in the ocean, and you know how rare we have that in our water. It's as though it flowed in for us. Then, we kissed.

"Oh, Debbie, I experienced the best kiss I've ever had. You know, the kind where they are fully present, giving, and un-rushed? Anyway, we ended up so far down the beach that we called a cab to get back to my car. I swung him by his house, where I exercised restraint, as you suggested. But I wanted so much to go in when he asked me. I remembered what you said about moving too fast. Going slow wasn't easy; I wanted to be very unladylike and jump his bones. Now, I'm wondering if your advice was any good. Do you think I blew it? Do you think he still wants to be with me?"

"He called me this morning to thank me for you. He's as worried about how you think of him. I've never seen two people fall in love so fast; it's sweet and beautiful."

Chapter 16

Sam

Africa is hot. Hot, hot, hot. Our vacation begins by checking into a boutique hotel, one of the older, original hotels —genuinely Afrikaner, unlike the modern resorts in Cape Town. I like this one. Crafts like red Zulu hats made by a local tribe hang on the wall. But Antelope rugs scattered on the wood floor? I'm disgusted until I learn that local tribes eat their meat. If it isn't trophy hunting, I'm okay. Still, studying the wildlife heads mounted in the dining room isn't for me like it is for Charlotte.

She considers each one, naming each animal and spouting information about its habitat with the owner as I fill out the paperwork for our check-in. Char must have studied African wildlife for hours while I read travel brochures about shopping. She handled the details and insisted on arranging everything. Although the hotel looks pretty, I'm disappointed there is no masseuse. After lugging suitcases off the baggage carousel, I had hoped for a massage before lunch and before the tours begin tomorrow.

And Char's control issues bug me already.

"Sam, let's stay on the move to acclimate to the time change and make sure we sleep well on our first night here."

"Yeah. Okay. Good idea. I want to enjoy the sea

view, walk through the shops, and find a nice restaurant."

"Sam, we need to supply. We can eat afterward."

"Aiya. We just get here. Besides, we bought everything at home. What more do you need?"

Char buys seven shorts and seven tank tops in the same khaki color. The expensive trekking boots she bought at home look too hot, but Charlotte insists she wants to break them in.

"Sam, I hope you brought comfortable clothes. We aren't here to pick up pretty boys … or girls. It will be hot and dusty."

"What? Of course, I packed comfortable outfits; okay, maybe not like you just bought. But I like stylish, so people don't peg me as a geek every time. I'll be fine."

Curiosity gets the best of me while Char showers. I check her luggage. The sundresses Blair had bought disappeared. I find military-grade binoculars, canteens, and a compass in their place. I keep my mouth shut because I don't want a confrontation. I will find out everything … eventually.

Char finds a charming restaurant serving Dutch, French, Indian, and Malaysian flavors. I'm thinking of romance, but then, over a vegan dinner, she hands me a printed schedule of our itineraries.

"Here, Sam. Stick to this schedule. Read it. Learn it."

The plan includes "alone" time. Okay, she is overdue for privacy, but I don't want to be alone.

Unfortunately for her, the hotel booked us in a single-bedroom suite, expecting a man and a woman, Sam and Charlotte. I like the cozy suite on the second floor with turn-of-the-century decor mixed with modern pieces. I love the Juliette balcony overlooking the park, too. But Char focuses on the one bed and calls the desk to complain.

Her frown tells me they are full; we can't change rooms. I keep my thoughts to myself as we share a King-size bed. She is Little Sis, after all, family.

I study Char while she sleeps, remembering when Blair suggested a trip for a graduation gift. Little Sis surprised all of us with a passion never seen before, choosing South Africa in a nano-second. She bloomed like a rose after that but continued with thorns and all. It's just a phase. After all, it would be her first separation from Blair in over three years.

Still, everyone was glad to see her and her new attitude go —everyone but me. I couldn't bear it, so I invited myself along. Char tensed up immediately, but Blair was thrilled.

"How wonderful." I provided a solution to her worry about Char going alone. In my heart, I knew she didn't want my company—it stung, too. But I hoped she would grow into the idea and even come to want me around. I still hope for that.

The prospect of our trip broke her shell into bits. She stood taller, and her step went from a ghostly walk behind her sister to a stride that left Blair behind.

Blair's nerves got the best of her. She counted the days until Charlotte's trip.

"She's growing up, so let her go. It's long overdue."

"Sam, I understand, but something is off. It's like she's angry at something...no—angry at me. Don't you feel the difference in her?"

"Of course, there's a change. Char shadowed your every move and tagged along with you and all of us. That's not who you want her to be forever, do you? Well, do you? Her behavior is healthy. She's twenty-one years old. Get off her back."

Debbie and Meghan agreed with me one hundred percent, but Blair was too close to Char's emotional oddities to see it. She finally kept her snide comments about Char's transformation to herself. That helped to change her own attitude fast. She seemed happier when she let go of her concerns about Charlotte. She stopped wearing a prisoner's uniform. Now, she reminds me of the Blair I met in college—self-assured and determined but light-hearted.

Since we experienced our first GNO, everyone has had a magical makeover. Meghan found another Mr. Right while Debbie stopped fooling around behind Greg's back. Blair still waits to discover her man, and now that she acts more like the old Blair, love will find her.

I try to face my truth. Charlotte has stolen my heart, but I keep my feelings to myself. She is family, so I enjoy our friendship and treat her like a peer. I think she appreciates my respect, but does she suspect my true feelings?

Oh, the tirades we shared about animal abusers and what we would do if we got our hands on them. Her eyes tell me she would kill them if given half a chance. I'd be at her side helping if she would let me. We shared the same passion. But Meghan always talks about the process of law and the civilized way to handle things.

"Civilized. Why should civilized laws pertain to evil people and killers who murder an elephant for its tusk? Why? I say fuck them," our new, outspoken Char said.

"We would be no better than the abuser if we took matters into our own hands," Meghan explained.

"Maybe that's what is needed. A champion to fight the enemies on their playing field."

Little hairs on the back of my neck raised when I heard it. But you know how things are. We push stuff out of our minds because we don't want to believe it; we refuse to see it. I guess that's what I do with Char to this day. Yeah, I'm sure of it. I become sleepy while feeling chills, wanting a smaller bed, wishing for more.

****

Char's voice commands me in a dream. "Hurry, Sam. No time for you to shower."

I jolt awake. "It's still dark outside." I stretch and yawn, realizing I never studied the itinerary. I'm miffed that I was too tired to shower last night.

"We fly to the lodge in time for the first safari of the day. Don't worry. The rest of the days in Africa won't require you to get up so early. Hustle, now."

I grumble as I dress and lather up with sunblock, suggesting that Char does the same.

"I'm telling you for the last time…I don't burn."

There's no arguing with her. With all the skin exposed in her tank and shorts, she will learn the hard way. She stuffs a cap in her back pocket and wears a shirt around her waist.

Look at her! She's changed over the past year. Her sinewy tendons look like a runner's outlined with supple muscles. Her figure reached perfection without her usual baggy clothes—her legs travel miles into her ankle-high boots. Her beautiful black hair hangs down without restraint over a Khaki tank that she wears braless, thanks to her small breasts.

A metamorphosis happened—Char left the cocoon, but is she a harmless butterfly? At this point, in this place, I don't know her at all.

Char stores all unnecessary items in the hotel where we will spend our last night in South Africa. She carries an oversized backpack with her new clothes and a small duffle with gear inside. I put up with her overwhelming pace, offering some advice when necessary.

"I hope you packed tampons just in case. You never know if the change in schedule changes your cycle."

"I don't have a cycle."

"What? You are too young not to bleed. What do you mean? You don't have periods?"

"Let it go, Sam."

"But it isn't natural. You are young. Are you sick? Oh my God, you must be sick…"

"I'm not sick, but I never want children. I took care of it medically this past year. I no longer have a cycle; now, let the topic go. I don't want to hear another word. Do you understand?"

"Sure. Yeah, okay. I will let it go." One day, I will learn why she did something so silly because I don't let go so quickly.

She hangs her fancy binoculars around her neck and puts on her khaki cap. "Let's go," she commands, and I jump to attention. She grabs her backpack and the near-empty duffel. Maybe it is for souvenirs, but there is no time to ask. We hustle across the hotel's lobby as I roll my suitcase behind. For this trip with Char, I paid attention to every hair, to the color of my lip gloss and nails. I look cute in my light denim short shorts with a matching top. But when heads turn, they stare at Char, not me. Without a stitch of makeup, she is stunning…her walk means business. I am proud to be seen with her.

The Biggest Five private tour company collects us

before the sun is up. A man wearing a jungle hat holds up Char's name, and she beelines to him. We make our introductions, and the driver explains the itinerary.

"That's all your bags, ladies? I never saw women pare their stuff down to so little, let alone two women."

Then he sees my large suitcase. "Oh, I spoke too soon."

Char is irritated. "We brought what we needed for the safari. Period. You are providing the water and transportation, correct?"

"Ah, yes, ma'am, I'm just impressed. Most ladies over-pack for the occasion, but I see you understand safaris more than most. That makes travel more manageable for all of us. He nods approvingly at Char's boots while judging my white sneakers with doubt.

"You don't expect them to stay white, do you?" He snickers as he holds the door open for me.

"Aiya. Good that I brought two pairs along." *He better mind his own business, or I'll give him a piece of my mind.* Finally, the Land Rover cruises out of the city to a regional airport.

Char holds on to her backpack and duffel as two men take my roll-along, looking through the car for more. The guide says something with that thick Afrikaner accent, and they smile. As soon as the driver points out our small four-seater plane, Char starts shouting orders.

"Let's go; there won't be time for dawdling here. Keep up, or I will leave you behind."

"Aiya. I'm coming. My legs are shorter than yours, you know." She bosses me like an impossible husband.

I try keeping up with her gazelle-like stride, but will I ever keep pace with Char's anxieties? I want to spend my leisure time like a real tourist. But her mind is in overdrive as we board the plane—a small plane. She knew I hated small planes when she booked the tour. But I can't show fear or complain; Char might leave me behind and go on the tour alone. Then, everyone will be mad at me.

I shake but take a deep breath and climb in. As we taxi down the runway, I say, "Don't be so mean to me. I want to have a good time, too, and little planes scare me."

Char stares at me and takes a deep breath. "Sorry, Sam. Sorry, but I meant what I said."

The engines roar as the plane lifts into the air. I white-knuckle the whole trip, wondering what I have gotten myself into traveling with Charlotte Innocenti.

Chapter 17

We watch the sunrise from the air and land outside Greater Kruger Park. I'm not awake without my coffee. Char wants us to tour so many preserves, and this is an awful start to her ambitious itinerary. We store our bags in the lodge. At least it is charming, with a thatched roof and an interior of natural wood and stone.

The bedroom contains two beds, and my heart sinks just a bit.

"Come on, Sam. Safari starts in minutes."

As we sprint toward the lobby, I clear my throat. "Char, I haven't had coffee, and I'm starving." Thank goodness the guide hears me.

"Better eat full up, ladies, yeah? You've got thirty minutes at the buffet, take care of the toilet, and then we're off. We are running a bit late, anyway. Oh, and if you are munchers, we'll bring plenty of trail mix. Anything else, bring from the breakfast table. Nothing that melts, or it'll be a mess in minutes. We provide the essentials."

A buffet? It seems spare to me—lots of fruits and bread. At Char's urging, I eat quickly, grabbing a large coffee to go.

"You may want to try the tea here, Sam."

"Aiya. You know me and my coffee. Don't worry." I quickly learn that this economical resort serves lousy coffee—weak like brown water. "You weren't kidding,

Char. This coffee tastes like bitter nothing."

"I tried to tell you; next time, listen."

The guide introduces himself. "I'm Hank, your guide for the next couple of days. You must be Samantha and Charlotte?"

I correct him, "I'm Sam. She's Charlotte."

"Oh, got it. Right then, ladies, always keep your hands in the vehicles. No loud laughter, certainly no screaming."

He smiles at the face I make when he says, *screaming*. I am a little scared. People ogle us as we climb into a small four-wheel drive, not the bigger ones that carry eight or more passengers.

"Why do we have a little car instead of those big ones?" I ask the guide.

"Your friend, Charlotte, ordered a private tour—up close and personal."

A native Afrikaner climbs onto the front seat, startling me. He carries a high-powered gun and a belt with lots of ammo.

"Ah, you need that gun? Is this trip so dangerous?" My voice squeals when I worry, and I'm worried.

"It isn't a gun, Sam; it's a rifle," Char explains like I bothered her already.

The driver eases my mind. "No concerns, Samantha. Insurance requires protection always, but no worries. Meet Shaka—guide and protector."

To my surprise, Char cuts off the guide's introduction and breaks out in some language I can't understand. The native with the rifle smiles and talks back, pointing to parts of his rifle as he replies in the same language. She continues asking questions. Shaka answers. The only word I understand is when Shaka says, "Russian."

Shaka smiles approvingly at Char. "You will make this safari more interesting than usual."

I elbow Char. "Any more surprises? I mean, you never talk, well, hardly ever, but you can break out in gibberish…"

"Not gibberish, Sam, Swahili."

"And perfect Swahili, too," Shaka adds in a deep voice.

"Do you know more than to talk about guns and…"

"Again, it's a rifle," Char says through clenched teeth.

"Aiya. Rifle, okay. But you want to tell me any more about the things you learned for this trip? Or do you plan to surprise me by the minute?"

"Observe and learn. Now, stop the chit-chat and start enjoying."

I like chit-chatting.

The dusty road kicks up a cloud of brown, but it isn't too bumpy. We slow down and come to a stop next to a sleeping lion pride.

"If you want to photograph, now is the time to do it," the guide whispers, and his caution scares me.

"Oh." I rattle around in my bag to pull out my new phone to photograph.

"Sh." Char shushes me.

Hank's hushed voice tells us about the lions prowling at night and that they probably just laid down to rest. Usually tech-savvy, I fumble with my phone because I don't like being so close to a dangerous animal. As I take photos, I see an eye open.

"Oh, oh. Char, a big lion, opened its eye." I whisper in a low voice because I want to live.

The guide answers my concerns. "Lions can't distinguish us from the car, Sam. They are used to cars. The best thing to do is to watch their tails. If a lioness or lion starts switching it back and forth, we leave…quickly."

Shaka turns his head away, laughing at me, and I don't like it.

"What? You think I'm so funny, huh? I never see lions like this. You make fun of my fear, asshole?"

"Sam, quiet." Char shakes my shoulder.

"Well, little lady, your loud, angry voice pissed off a lion, the big male."

"Oh, oh. Driver, he comes toward me. Please, go now!" I cower behind his seat.

The driver takes off, but not before the lion's roar rattles my eardrum. "Hey, you drive too fast."

We round the corner when the driver slams on the brakes.

"Listen, miss. If you can't control yourself, you won't be traveling on safari with this lodge. I will not endanger my life, Shaka's, or Charlotte's. If you want to offer yourself as a meal, go right ahead, but do it on your own time, not mine. My record is perfect. Twenty years—I've never lost one person to a wild animal attack. Until today, I've never even come close. You keep your mouth shut, are we clear?"

Charlotte glares at me, and I feel sorry to cause such a scene. "Okay. I will be quiet. I put a zipper on my lips. Sorry."

Char ignores my apology. "She got the message, Hank. Let's move on."

True to my word, I say nothing else for the rest of that safari. I concentrate on taking photos of zebras, giraffes, and a pack of elephants with babies. The elephant family crosses the road in front of us and behind us. I stay quiet by biting my finger.

****

Hank confronts me when we're back at the lodge. "I'm sorry I disciplined you, Miss. I quite appreciate your ah…braveness for the remainder of the safari. I'll see you two this afternoon."

As he walks away, Charlotte chastises me. "Sam, not one word to management about Hank being rude or anything like that. You did put us all in danger, but you won't do that again, will you?"

Charlotte fixes her attention on me in a way I have never experienced before. Her assertiveness scares me as she towers over me, but I like it, too. Will I ever get used to it?

"No, Char. I promise, but what's this about going out again this afternoon?"

"Sam, safaris are twice a day. In between, you can eat, cool off in the pool, read, or do whatever you want. There's Wi-Fi here, too. The restaurant serves breakfast right now."

"Breakfast again? Good, my fucking stomach needs to stop the rumble."

"The first meal holds you over on morning Safari. The lodge offers a full menu after the safari. The next meal is between two and three; if you read the brochure, you'd know that. Pace yourself; safari again at four."

"All right then, let's eat." She nods, but her expression says that I disappoint her. My heart hurts over it. "I'll be better on safari, I promise."

Char relaxes a bit. "I know you will try. In the future, if you would rather be pampered at the lodge instead of joining me on safari, feel free to do so. I want to concentrate on my surroundings without worrying about you."

"Really? You worry about me?" My heart flutters, but she responds with nothing. "If you don't mind, I'll take that offer. You sure don't need me to look after you."

"That's an improvement. I'm glad you realize that. This lodge employs masseuses. Why don't you get one this afternoon while I'm on safari?"

"Yeah? That's a good surprise. I feel jet-lagged; a massage would help." I can't believe my stroke of good luck.

"We won't be staying in three-star lodges the whole time. I took what was available. But I booked the last two nights at The Four Seasons for you. You can stay in the room to see the big five; it overlooks the watering hole."

"The Four Seasons? Oh, now you speak my language. Thank you! That sounds more like my kind of safari."

"I thought so."

I begin to understand that Char is the chaperone, and I am the student, but I don't mind one bit. I rescue dogs, cats, horses, and all farm animals, but this African environment throws me. When I see an elephant mama and her baby, when I understand the slaughter of the animals, I'll give in any way possible to save them. But I want to do it from the comfort of my computer, back home in Florida, in suburbia, with no lions roaring.

But Char worries about me and thinks of me. Maybe, one day, we will share something more than a safari.

****

I'm happy to take Char's advice and book a masseuse for an hour in the afternoon. But can anyone release the tension my muscles feel around Char? Meanwhile, I eat my fill of fresh fruits and veggies. She eats even more sparingly and concentrates on her iPad.

"What's so interesting?"

Char is irritated that I interrupted. "Fauna, Sam. There's a nature walk after breakfast; I want to prepare."

"I want to stretch my legs, too. Am I invited?" Char wants to say something snarky; I can feel it. Her expression isn't at all inviting, but she says, "Of course."

****

Maybe Char's knowledge of plants is a compulsive thing. But something more must be going on. She identifies local fauna in conversation with the guide, spouting off facts about each thorny bush or flower. What's the point of remembering all that when we never will see them again? Something doesn't make sense to me.

After the nature walk, I change into my skimpiest bikini and dive into the pool's deep end, holding my breath forever while my brain works overtime to try to understand Char. What is driving her? When my lungs feel like they are going to explode, I burst to the surface the way sea turtles do in the Intracoastal back home. I catch a breath and submerge again to think about her some more until I wear myself out. Then, I swim a few laps, stretching muscles I never use at the computer.

Meanwhile, Char sits in the shade, fixating on whatever is on her screen and ignoring me. I lather on more sunscreen and choose a spot to relax with my Kindle. Maybe she is obsessive/compulsive. From what I've seen, this Charlotte is a genius, maybe a savant, and

I'm impressed by how she hid it from everyone for years.

I'm glad she has stepped out of her shell, but the intensity of the information pouring out of her mouth worries me. Yet, I'm not sure why I'm concerned.

"I know you just graduated, Char, but have you considered a master's or a doctorate? Your love for this country and its animals could be in your future—animal husbandry or major in African culture."

"Yes, you're right," she says irritably. "I'll think about that when we get home, but while we're here, I want to feel this environment without thinking about tomorrow, okay?"

"Aiya, Char. I'm just making conversation…"

"I don't want conversation; do you get that now?"

I hold my temper and obey her demand for silence, but I lose Char today. She lives somewhere unreachable, although I sit right by her. Maybe she needs medication. Calling Blair is impossible; I refuse to admit I can't "handle" Char. I can never own that… too much pride, I guess. Anyway, controlling someone is wrong. The Star Trek writer Gene Roddenberry coined a phrase I adopted: "Do not interrupt the prime directive." So, I don't interfere with Char's direction, no matter how unsettling. Besides, she doesn't show signs of danger to anyone. How can her newfound independence be wrong?

****

This morning, we move from our lodge to gorilla trekking in the Congo. I like this part. We sit quietly as Momma and the babies amble by, ignoring us. I sit close to the guide without fear ruling me, like on the first safari with man-eaters.

From here, we travel to Uganda. As Char goes off on another Safari, I find a conservation park dedicated to wounded animals that can't be returned to the jungle. I adore holding a baby lion in my arms. But I get mad again when I see an orphaned baby elephant with part of his trunk missing. My feelings change directions all the time. I soar when I bottle-feed a baby baboon; I fall in love with its cuteness. But when I hear of all their mothers murdered by farmers when they steal crops, I'm sad again. My emotions climb and fall like a non-stop roller coaster, but Africa has inched into my heart. When I get home, I will donate to the parks that help these orphans.

I lose track of flights, countries, and the excessive information I hear. Our vacation touches South Africa only, but poaching exists throughout the continent. I don't understand how they can get away with it. But my new awareness of Char's brilliance grips me. When I'm not surprised at her intellect, I am in awe of her determination.

Blair's genius manifests with numbers. Period. But Char's intelligence is more profound, broader, and darker. She senses the interconnectedness of everything. Maybe she always did, but I never saw it until we traveled here together. Still, the intensity is too much— way too much. I want to leave after the second week together.

Char is not a person anymore; she's a computerized robot, taking in information and ejecting it to the guides. This stranger makes me feel lonely and homesick.

I'm eager to cross-post Africa's needs when I return home. Still, I will miss the people and animals I met from this beautiful continent's conservation and animal rights groups. My emotions are still up and down, and I can't wait for the ride to end.

Chapter 18

Charlotte

"Will you miss Africa, Sam?" I already know her answer.

"African people and rescue animals, yes. Safari, no. I breathed enough dust and bumped enough of my insides. And I don't like being in a place where men with guns protect me. That's your thing. But I love seeing the rescues here, holding baby cheetahs and baboons. I love that the best."

"Rifles, Sam. Rifles. They didn't use them once, did they?"

"No, that's true. But you know how I feel about rifles, even after shooting lessons. I'm ready to go home and begin supporting Africa safely from my computer. Aren't you ready to leave?"

I tell Sam a partial truth. "I learned all I needed to learn—South Africa is variable."

"What variables?"

"Languages, dialects, and customs constantly fluctuate when traveling. Animals and fauna change, too, and we concentrated only on South Africa for this trip. It would take a great, adaptable mind to understand the basic characteristics of all the cultures, geography, and animals unless they spent a lifetime focusing on African studies." *And I have a lifetime.*

"Let's get some sleep. You'll want to buy out Cape Town tomorrow. That should wear you out for the flight home."

I don't share that I love this place, this continent, or that I feel at home in the wild, part of the predator/prey cycle. One more day with Sam, then I'll be free to commit my life to Africa. I dream of Sam at the airport, telling her goodbye. "I'm staying. I'm a species savior who will make a difference."

"Good for you. You destroy those poachers. Find those warlords and slit their throats. You save all the animals in Africa, not just the tusked ones."

When I wake, I'm disappointed. The dream is a delusion because Sam would try to tackle me to the ground and call the police to bring me home. I don't begrudge Sam her feelings. As my angelic messenger, she had brought the plight of all animals into my consciousness. She had given me my purpose, a release from my unusual thought patterns that were full of anger and not going anywhere productive. I don't envy her the burden of telling Blair of my impending disappearance. In a way, it makes her a co-conspirator in my plans. One day, I will let her know that she is a hero!

We spend the last day walking in and out of colorfully painted shops with quaint European architecture. Sam buys gifts for her friends and souvenirs for her apartment. Finally, she has learned not to ask me why I'm not interested in purchasing anything.

The lights, the traffic, and the sound of people everywhere insult my system. I've already acclimated to the jungles, the grasslands, and the great outdoors. I practice breathing to endure the endless shops that Sam enjoys.

Tonight, I will watch my past take off from the tarmac.

****

Sam

I call Blair from the Miami airport and accept her panic that erupts like a burst gas main. Boom!

"What do you mean Char is missing? You are with her. You're supposed to be with her all the time!"

"Aiya! I was, Blair. We ate dinner together. We waited for the flight and had drinks, but then she told me."

"What exactly did she say? Think! For God's sake, think!"

I take a deep breath before answering to keep from tuning in to Blair's hysterics! My heart pounds and my throat tightens.

"Charlotte said she arranged to sit in a different plane section. She wanted freedom and time alone to think about her African experience. She changed seats without my knowing it. And she chose to sit in the back of the plane, as far from first class and me as possible.

"What did you want me to do, girlfriend? You know how headstrong she is. She wanted to be alone. What could that hurt on the trip home, I thought? So, I didn't fuss at her. After all, she spent the whole day shopping with me, and you know she hates shopping. Then we arrived at the airport together and checked in together.

"We said goodbyes at the gate because I boarded first. Char's section boarded in the rear. It never occurred to me she wouldn't get on the flight, so I didn't look for her. Now I'm sorry I didn't check."

"Are you sure she didn't get on?"

"I confirmed with the airlines. Char told them she had an emergency and canceled her seat. I'm sorry, Blair."

"At least we know she left of her own volition and wasn't kidnapped. I'll call Debbie; she'll know what to do. Her detective will find Char; she has to."

I know frantic when I hear it. "She must have had her reasons."

"No reason is good enough. Charlotte knows I'll worry to death over her. Now, I understand why she seemed so mysterious all these months. Whatever her agenda, she wanted to keep us on the outs. She's alone on a strange continent, a young woman surrounded by jungles and jungle people, and..."

"Aiya. Blair, stop. Char is not as helpless as you think; I saw it firsthand. Your sister knows what she is doing. That Little Sis of yours is smarter than any of us...all of us put together. She's beyond an ordinary genius. She's like a savant or something."

"What are you saying? My Char?"

"Yes, your Char. I don't know why she tricked us for so long or what her plans were, but she learned about every animal, plant, and tribe that we interacted with. She even speaks a few languages no one ever heard of in America. Listen, I'm boarding for the final leg home, but I wanted to let you know right away. I'll see you in Jacksonville. Have faith."

"Easy for you to say. She's not your sister."

No, Char isn't my sister, but I hate losing her. It hurts me all the same.

Oddly, I'm not worried about her one bit.

****

African Continental Convention - Ten years later

"…Yes. I represent only South Africa. Many of you, rulers of independent countries, don't agree with our democracy, opinions, or ideologies. Many dignitaries have traveled great distances to attend this meeting in a new modern trade complex that will bring us together more often. Today, we set aside our differences.

"We leaders gather to discuss many issues, but I must first bring up what my heart decides is the most crucial topic. It is a shared problem that is also a blessing.

"Someone called Duma dedicates their life to protecting African wildlife. First alone, but for the past decade or more, our tribal women have united and have followed this protectorate of Africa, calling themselves The Defenders. We admit that the Defenders use illegal methods to achieve positive results against poachers. Through arms and militia, they have achieved more than we and individual states have managed through legal means.

"Protected Elephant and Rhino populations have increased. Ape species are growing. Poachers are dead or on the run. The Defenders achieved what the vast continent had failed to do for decades. They do not divulge their names. They seek no glory and avoid prosecution.

"We are confident The Defenders loathe politics and power, so they will not usurp our political systems. They only eliminate unwanted threats to our animal populations. As such, tourism has increased, and the only allowable shooting on most of the continent is with a photo lens. The Defenders enforce that law across our beautiful Africa. Anonymous women, mothers, and young ladies take up arms against poachers and evildoers. Although some have died for their cause, many more have risen to take their place.

"A few of you request that The Defenders be stopped and prosecuted. But I refuse to obstruct them as they have shown the eliminated have proved to be in the wrong. Ladies and gentlemen, a good tree does not bear bad fruit.' The Defenders is a good tree.

Today, when we vote on whether or not to condemn The Defender's actions, I must vote nay. Let us join today to all vote nay. This is not a vote for illegal activity or violence. It is merely a vote to ignore The Defenders until we, as a continent, can oversee the good they have accomplished and until the governments create uncorrupt systems to prevent poaching more effectively than in the past.

"Again, I vote Nay, for now. Let us join as a continent and ignore The Defenders until a better time. Thank you."

Chapter 19

Debbie

Fifteen years after Char's disappearance - Amelia Yacht Club

I'm the sick puppy, yet I'm the first to arrive, as usual. Greg orders a club soda for me before leaving. He's reading the riot act to the staff about my having no alcohol, it being a matter of life and death. I can't get away with a darn thing anymore.

"Debbie?" Meghan stands with Sam next to her. I didn't see them coming. They hug me like I'm a rare piece of China. By the expression on their faces, I must appear puny despite my best effort with makeup and blush to cover my jaundiced skin.

"Didn't Blair warn you that I don't look my best these days?"

"Yeah."

Meghan elbows Sam.

"Don't poke me. I'm telling the truth because we're all friends here. She said your speech is slower, but you are still clever and beautiful."

"Thanks, Sam, for your honesty. It's the transfusions that slow my speech."

Blair sashays in but sighs when she spots me. She gives me a sweet kiss on the cheek.

"This is as good a place as any to reunite, Debbie." She hugs Sam and Meghan.

"Don't look at me; I didn't choose it. I thought one of you did."

Someone speaks before we figure out why we're at a meeting that not one of us arranged.

"I called you together, ladies." A soft, South African accent sounds from behind us. A handsome man about six feet with cropped black hair, a trimmed mustache, and rich tan wearing resort-chic clothes strides toward us. Sam's mouth drops open, speechless.

"Hell's bells. Who in heaven's name are you?" I ask.

"He looks…familiar." Blair squints at the stranger.

"I am someone from your past, someone from long ago who wants to thank you."

"Thank us for what?" Meghan asks suspiciously.

"You spoke many years ago about animal rights…enacting laws to protect animals. It changed my life forever."

Sam inhales loudly. All eyes turn to her. "So, you became a part of the solution?"

"At the expense of possible arrest, in this country as well as others, yes."

The rugged, muscular man stands comfortably— hand in one pocket, expressive with the other one.

"You…. you began The Defenders?" Sam's eyes begin to tear up.

"Yes, Sam. I did."

How can he know Sam's name? Suddenly, she jumps into the stranger's arms, crying silently. He smiles and wraps his arms around her.

"You are alive. I knew it. I knew it."

"My God, Char?" Meghan exclaims. "Is it you?"

He puts a finger to his lips. "Sh."

Blair and I slowly push back our chairs, studying and shaking our heads. I finally see it, but I can't fully believe it. Meanwhile, tears well in Blair's eyes as she approaches the stranger carefully.

"You? You are my Char?" She says with a hint of disgust.

"Allow me to introduce myself... My name is Charles. Charles Innocenti."

Blair glares at him. "How dare you? How? Why? I finally gave up hope, thinking you were dead."

"I am sorry, really, I am, but please lower your voice. The law is watching closely, you know."

Sam stomps her foot. "Blair, stop. Charles is an international hero. Do you know how many lives he saved?"

"Him? He's, she's not him, she's Char." Blair betrays another tinge of repugnance in her voice. Everyone is so emotional, but I don't have the energy for it, so I sit down.

"You wondered why I was so quiet, Blair." He holds his arms out, displaying the man in the suit. "This is why. Those days, those times persecuted people like me. But this person that stands before you has always existed."

"Oh, Jesus. Now, what do I do with this information?" Blair buries her face in her hands.

Age has mellowed Sam's temper, and she only growls softly. "Maybe you can welcome a family member home? One who most people would be proud to call brother?"

"I don't know what to say. I'm so angry at you for disappearing because I sent you on that trip. I believed it was all my fault." Blair looks tormented, conflicted by her emotions.

"Sis, it wasn't anyone's fault. Destiny called, and I followed it."

Blair falls into his arms, sobbing, smacking his shoulder in protest, and hugging Charles again. I sit silently while taking it all in.

He smiles and holds her. "I'm fine, but I must accomplish more. Vigilance is essential."

"What do you mean 'accomplish more'? You are home now."

"I can't stay anywhere for too long, ladies. Please, let's stop calling attention to ourselves and sit down." Charles holds a chair out for his sister. "I thought enough time had passed that none of you could be implicated in my schemes and actions, especially once the law considered Charlotte dead."

Meghan sits rigidly at the age of her seat, ready to pounce. "You may be a hero to animal lovers and environmentalists, Charles, but I know how many humans lost their lives promoting your agenda and protecting you."

"Ah, always the law, Meghan? Yes, that is true, but we eliminate those who intend or have murdered creatures for ivory tusks, never anyone innocent."

"Murder is murder. And some of the women you recruited died."

"As African mothers, not only of human children but also all of Africa, they understood their dangerous missions and volunteered. If you like, I shall recite the names of our dead warriors for you right now." Charles's eyes, like Samurai swords, slice through Meghan's self-righteousness. She doesn't back down.

"So, why return to us? Really? What is your agenda

now?"

The face-off continues.

"I'm here for multiple reasons. One, I missed my sister… and Sam. I wanted to say thank you for helping to make me who I am."

"And what else, Charles? Exactly, what else?"

"I thought we could enjoy a pleasant dinner and exchange stories, Meghan. But you've made that quite impossible, haven't you?"

I'm tired of the drama. "Charles, I'm happy you are alive, but Meghan senses you are here for reasons beyond a social visit. I only have so much energy, so let's get to it, shall we, darlin'?"

"I need funds to carry The Defenders into the future. Remember, you are the one who brought me, and all of us, into our first awareness."

"What are you talking about?"

"Seth Overmeyer. Remember? The atrocity that gave all of us focus."

"Into focus? Or into insanity?" Meghan snaps.

"Enough, Megs. You speak to my sister, my brother, now. My brother." Blair repeats as if to set the change within her mind. "And, yes, we were all adamant about making a difference back then, and we have. Now, animal abusers end up on an FBI list of offenders. But nobody effected more change than Charles. He made the entire world take notice. Elephant and rhino populations have risen for the past fifteen years, and sports hunting is gone, thanks to my brother."

"So, you don't care how he did it?" Meghan strikes snake-like.

"No need to attack me, girlfriend. But, no, how The Defenders achieve their excellent results is bothersome, but only good has come of it." Blair stands her ground like a defiant bull elephant—I'm proud of her.

Meghan's hands curl into fists. "Good? The Defenders movement is taking place here in America. We want animal abusers to serve jail time and get psychological help. Now, they end up dead before trial. Do you think that doesn't have anything to do with your brother's vigilantism? Watchdogs run rampant now, thanks to him."

Charles shakes his head and holds up a finger. "Those that kill in the United States are rogues—not a part of The Defenders. I'm not privy to those events, nor do I sanction them."

Sam stands, pointing at Meghan. "Aiya, maybe they did what was needed. Maybe we don't have all the facts. Maybe, the assholes that got killed in the U.S. needed to disappear."

"I will not be a part of this insane conversation or this company." Meghan jumps out of her chair and storms out like a Florida hurricane.

Charles maintains his coolness. Years of jungle life must have taught him the importance of containing one's emotions. "Hmm, rather dramatic for an attorney, don't you think?"

"I'd say. I've never seen Meghan that angry or react that way. It is disturbing, and I don't care for it," Blair says.

"So, let's forget Meghan and return to the topic. How much do you need, Charles?" I ask.

"It's substantial. Certainly, I don't expect you to foot the bill. But if you can gather all your well-monied friends together with a benefit, perhaps you can convince them to open their wallets to support The Defender's next challenge, human trafficking—again protecting the innocent."

I'm surprised. "Human trafficking? Oh. Yes, I can see The Defenders being effective in that arena. Human trafficking needs a quicker solution than law enforcement provides. Little boys and girls are trapped into soliciting their bodies, enslaved for sex. Yes. I'll help all I can. It's about time people stand up for what is right, no matter how uncomfortable the topic."

"I appreciate that, Debbie. Now, having said what I came to say, I'll be off, but I'll be in touch."

"What? No dinner? You aren't coming home to meet my husband and your niece and nephew?" Blair whines, but I understand her disappointment.

"Thanks to Meghan, the danger level has increased for me. I kept track of you through the years, if it's any consolation. Remotely, I watched you become Mrs. Albert Finney. I knew the moment you gave birth, both times. Thank you for naming Charlotte after me. You created a beautiful family. But Meghan may have contacted the authorities. I can't stay."

"Aiya. She wouldn't." Sam says lividly.

"Yes, she would. You better go quickly," I suggest.

"Sam, I'll be in touch to find out the particulars about the benefit if that's okay." Charles pushes away from the table and stands.

"Okay? I've been waiting fifteen years for you to contact me directly. Of course, it's okay."

Charles nods and quickly disappears out a side door.

Sam heaves a sigh as if her heart is splintering.

Blair looks confused. "Sam… what do you mean you waited for Charles to contact you directly?"

Sam looks sheepish. "Listen, Blair, I've contributed

to The Defenders for years. Many times, I received messages that sounded too familiar, as though the person that sent them knew me."

"And you didn't tell me? How could you not tell me?"

"Shh, Blair. I wasn't sure if my heart played games because I wanted it to be true or if it was real. Maybe my imagination made something that was not there. I couldn't do that to you, adding an extra measure of misery."

"That makes sense, Blair. You freaked for quite a few years over Char... I mean, Charles. Sam was right not to fan that flame."

"Yes, I suppose so. I understand, Sam; I do. And, now, I must adapt to him. I have a brother named Charles. What next?"

"Next, I throw together a gala to benefit The Defenders!"

"Debbie, you're ill. You need your strength, so let us help."

"Certainly not; I'm doing well enough. I've been on the liver transplant list for a couple of years. One will turn up at any time. Meanwhile, transfusions keep me going. Besides, benefit galas are my specialty. Most of it is email and phone work only. Let's toast to Blair's new brother; don't worry, I have club soda."

My friends pick up their water glasses.

"Don't abstain for my sake. I'm fine."

Blair shakes her head. "Battle of the Bulge, and I must keep up my strength with two kids."

Sam laughs. "I'm too happy to drink. Charles, our Charles is alive."

That he is, but I wonder how long that will last in the States?

Chapter 20

Meghan

My blood pressure is through the roof. My head hurts, and aspirin doesn't help. I clench and unclench my fists as I pace the floor in my modest galley kitchen for a solid hour. "The law is the law," I repeat over and over. It is my mantra that I believe more than anything. I center my life around that fact. Being true to myself means being loyal to the law. Rules knit society together, after all.

I think back to the days of Girl's Night Out that disbanded after husbands and children became a reality. I remember the boy Charles spoke about. Yes. Overmeyer. Seth Overmeyer, who killed the detective and another man. The teen whose suicide had never been challenged, a child snuffed out. Yet Charles, a killer on another continent, walks free. And the clothes he wore to meet us? They must have cost a fortune, and it irks me.

Seth. Charles. Why do those names keep repeating in my mind? Charles is an assassin; well, it is only a rumor; there is no direct evidence. But he motivates people to kill. Oh, what am I talking about? Everyone knows he executes poachers and warlords.

When did he begin to kill? Seth. Charles.

'We can hack into his computer…we can keep track.' Char said something like that, and Sam mentioned eliminating Seth. Sam mentored Char back then. What if Char took her words seriously? She couldn't have started killing that early, could she? But she wasn't Char then, either, was she? Charles lived back then, too.

I remember the look on Charlotte's face when we spoke of Seth, like she, no he, could kill him. My heart flutters; my stomach sinks. I reject the bolt of lightning that pierces my brain and my heart. No!

Blair Skyping us about the headlines in the morning paper flashes before me. What did it say? I search my memory. 'Local teen commits suicide,' or something like that. Blair had called too early because we had been out late the evening before, the night I met William. We all met nice men that night, except for Charlotte. She left early and took a cab home because she said she was sick. 'Don't wake me…do not wake me…do not wake me.'

"He did it. Charlotte, our little sis … no … Charles killed Seth Overmeyer." The truth washes through me like a tsunami, carrying bits of memories and facts. Why didn't I see it then? It seems obvious now.

Suddenly, I am afraid for my family. My gut conveys the truth, but the authorities must discover it. My fingers shake too much to Google.

"Siri, contact the local FBI."

"This is Mrs. Meghan Kent-Cooper, Public Defender for Nassau County, Florida. I have valuable information regarding a possible murder, a cold case. Yes. No, I do not want agents here. I have three children and a husband who could be in danger if the law comes to my front door. No meeting at my office either … Monday may be too late.

"Let's meet in your office tomorrow. Yes, I know it is Sunday; it is *that* important. It concerns the creator of the vigilante group, The Defenders, and a boy named Seth Overmeyer, who died some fifteen or so years ago. Yes, I know their leader's name. Do I have your attention now?

"Ten a.m.? Suite 257? I will be there. Meanwhile, I require protection for my entire household until then because we are in danger. We are speaking of Charles Innocenti here. Yes, he created The Defenders. Thank you, see what you can do and get back to me."

****

Sam

Debbie says it will take six weeks to arrange and hold the gala. Pulling it together for all her ambitious ideas would take a miracle in that short period. Maybe Deb is concerned about her health holding up for the task? But she won't admit it as she always needs to be in control. Maybe she has something to prove, and the gala gives her a reason to hold on. Holding on … I can relate to that because I can't stop thinking about Charles and can't wait to see him again.

****

Where is Charles? I dream of him after spending seven agonizing days and nights with no word. Pacing the floor doesn't help, so I head toward the kitchen. Maybe a glass of wine will calm me. I pour half a glass but realize that it won't do. I'm a mixture of sad and peeved. Tonight, I fill the glass to the brim. After a few large gulps, I relax until I hear a tapping at my bedroom door.

"Could it be?" I jog down the hall to my bedroom. "You better be friendly because I have a gun."

"Good, Sam. I'm proud of you." I love the South

African voice that responds. Sliding the door open quickly, I'm thrilled that it really is Charles.

"What are you doing out there? It's chilly. Come in. Come in."

Aiya. I'm feeling tipsy already.

"Sh. I can't stay long. Did Debbie arrange the date for the benefit?"

"Yes, six weeks from the night we all met at the club—Saturday night at the convention hall. Charles, please don't run away this time. Please stay; stay with me." The words, the pleas, spill from my heart and pop out of my mouth.

"Sam, Meghan alerted authorities, and the FBI knows I'm nearby. My people tell me I'm in danger. I shouldn't be here tonight, but I wanted to see you. I missed you all those years."

"Oh, Charles. I fell in love with you long ago, and my feelings haven't changed. Tell me how you feel about me, please?"

He stares into my eyes momentarily before he bends and places his lips on mine. Goosebumps rise as the kiss grows from sweet and tender to something more. Suddenly, Charles pulls away.

"Sam, I can't. I chose my road."

"I can come with you."

"No, you can't. I live in the bush most of the time. And I quite remember how tiresome you found Africa."

I hang my head. "Because you wouldn't share your heart with me back then."

"I still can't. I didn't expect you to be a martyr. Find someone who can love you the way you deserve."

"I tried. But they can't compare to what my heart feels for you."

"Now you know my feelings, but I can't act upon them as too much is at stake. I must go. But first, this is very important: tell Debbie that The Defenders established a 501k for donations in the Caymans. She'll find it online. Donors must make checks out to the 501k Caymans and only there."

Charles checks an incoming text. "They are on to me, Sam; I must be off. Remember to keep your lips zipped."

As quickly as Charles slips into my heart again, he steps out into the darkness. I'm both thrilled and disappointed. It's time for more wine while I relive the kiss I dreamed of through the years. My body pulsates with passion until the doorbell rings and yanks me back to reality.

"What? Ten at night?" *Did Charles forget something?* I let the deadbolt on and open the door a crack.

"Samantha Yu?"

"Yeah. Who are you, and why do you ring my doorbell this late at night?" My anger at Charles for leaving me rises to the surface.

The porch light shines at eye level to the visitor. "FBI, ma'am." The stranger thrusts a badge out, pushing it through the opening. "We'd like to talk to you."

"Yeah, okay, it looks real. But why do you want to talk to me? And at this fucking time of night?"

"Please, may we come in? We won't take up much of your time."

"I'm in my nightie. No, you can't come in. Aiya. What's so important?"

"Ms. Yu, do you remember the case of Seth Overmeyer?"

"Who?"

"Seth Overmeyer. He died over fifteen years ago, but we'd like to verify how he died."

"Oh, the boy killer. That was long ago—a very sick teenager. Committed suicide, didn't he?"

"We thought so, ma'am. But an informant shared information that has the FBI reopening the case."

"That's stupid. The crazy boy is long dead."

"But even sick boys have a right to justice, don't you agree?" the agent asks.

There they go again. The hairs on the back of my neck...

"Of course. What does this boy have to do with me?"

"We're here because we learned your friend Char, now Charles Innocenti, may have been the perpetrator."

"Perpetrator? You mean you think she killed that boy? Aiya. Little Sis would never hurt a flea. She was very quiet and shy."

"No, but perhaps Charles would have?" The agent is relentless, but I hold myself together.

"Ridiculous. Tell me what you want so I can go to sleep."

"Intelligence says Charles is hiding somewhere in your vicinity. We want you to contact us anytime, day or night, if he contacts you. We need to detain him for questioning."

"Oh, I see. You want me to snitch on someone who never bothers to say a word to me in fifteen years? He won't call."

"If he does, here's my card. Your friend, Meghan, notified us out of duty. We hope for your cooperation, too."

I take the card, but what else can I do? "Meghan. I should have known—big imagination. She hated Little Sis, too. Sure, sure. I'll call you if I hear from her, I mean him. But don't hold your breath. Now, may I go to bed? I have an early morning."

"Certainly, Ms. Yu. Thank you for your cooperation."

"Yeah, well, I'm a good American; what else am I supposed to do?" I want to slam the door in his face, but I don't need the FBI as enemies. Still, I know Charles has told me the truth. He did have to rush out the door.

Is my love in the shadows watching, wanting to return to me? He felt the passion and the desire that I felt; I know it. I can't sleep because Seth Overmeyer keeps going through my brain. Char, Charles, whoever wouldn't have done it. He couldn't have, could he?

Anyway, that Seth was a bad one. He deserved death. But did he?

Damn, Meghan. Damn her.

Chapter 21

Debbie

For the first time since my failing liver diagnosis, I feel sheer satisfaction and gratefulness. Designing the gala makes me feel healthy again; at least my mind still works. With everyone so interested in helping, my ego inflates to a healthier level. Helping The Defenders already rewards me.

"Sam, the entire town is attending The Defenders gala. Guests are planning to fly in for it. Haven't you heard a word from Charles? I'd like him to know."

"No. But I heard from the FBI when they came to my door days ago, searching for Charles Innocenti."

"What?"

"I told the FBI Charles won't bother calling me."

"How did the FBI know his name?"

"Meghan alerted them—doing her stupid duty, I guess."

"Meghan. Shame on her, but I thought she might cause trouble after we met with Charles. It's a good thing he left when he did."

"Debbie, I forgot to tell the FBI about that dinner meeting that wasn't. Come to think of it, Charles said you should deposit benefit money to The Defenders' 501K online, registered in the Cayman Islands. Please make all checks out to them only. But, Debbie, you can't get in trouble for this gala, can you?"

"You're confusing me, Sam. No, the law in this country doesn't want to arrest The Defenders' originator. And I can't be held culpable if you are worried about that. I checked with my attorney right away, but I appreciate your concern.

"I don't remember Charles saying a word about a 501K…"

Suddenly, Sam is testy. "Debbie, I'm not making it up; I remember exactly. So, tell your donors to write the checks to The Defenders 501K in the Cayman Islands only. If I hear from him, I'll tell him to talk to you directly, okay? Meanwhile, follow his instructions."

Sam hangs up on me. No one hangs up on me. "Hm. That's weird, Greg."

"Who were you talking to?"

"Sam."

"Yeah, I expect a conversation with her would be weird." Greg winks at me.

"Stop, Greg. Seriously, it's as though she didn't want to talk about Charles at all."

"Maybe she just didn't want to talk." Greg pours another club soda for me.

"She'd tell me if she couldn't talk. Sam is straightforward. No, something is off."

"Maybe you interrupted something…delicate, if you get my drift."

"She'd tell me that too, in full detail, unless she was hiding something… or someone."

"Like Charles?" Greg guesses.

"Exactly. Sam's been keeping to herself increasingly. I bet the Feds watch her every move."

"Including phone calls between Sam and…" Greg

doesn't get to finish his sentence.

"Me? Do you think they are listening to my conversations? Isn't that against the constitution?" I'm a little embarrassed that I'm not sure about all the recent government changes.

"Ever since nine-eleven, when Homeland Security stepped up their game, our citizen's rights have gone the way of the Dodo Bird, sweetheart."

The idea that anyone dares to encroach on my privacy irks me. "I'm not doing anything illegal. I'm merely sponsoring a gala for The Defenders. The public loves them."

"Yes, but not everyone knows Charle's background. He keeps a low profile in the group—a smart guy. But don't be surprised if the feds attend your gala too, discreetly, of course. Your attorneys are certain that donating to The Defenders is legal?" Greg hopes I understand the gravity of the situation. "Remember, Charles is wanted everywhere, despite The Defender's positive results. The law won't accept his methods in the States. Now that Meghan has given the authorities a bone, they could arrest him here for murder, even if he didn't do it. That will incapacitate his plans."

"Great. Don't let that leak, Greg. I don't want to lose donors before the event."

"You know me better than that, but this scenario explains Sam's standoffishness."

"Sure does. Remind me to thank my friend at the gala, darling."

"My pleasure, dear. Meanwhile, watch your phone conversations. Now, can I convince you to eat a bit more?" Greg has bone broth on the spoon and points it towards my mouth.

****

Blair

Gosh, I'm so over wondering about Charles's whereabouts. I need answers, and I figure Sam will know before anyone else. Her phone rings a long time before she answers.

"Hi, Blair."

"Hey, sweet lady, have you heard from Charles?"

"Aiya. Why does everyone call me about Charles? You are his sister!"

"Well, it's obvious you two have a bond despite being many years apart." Gee, what is she all touchy about?

"That's all in your head, Blair. Charles won't contact me. He doesn't care about me at all. You remember Char from long ago. If he contacts anyone, it will be his sister before me."

"You think so? At our surprise meeting, his goodbye seemed final; he left so quickly. Could he be back in Africa by now?"

"He is, probably. I'm sad he didn't bother with a goodbye to me."

"Well, maybe he contacted Debbie."

"No, I talked to Debbie, and she heard nothing from him. I think you are right, Blair. He's back on the continent doing his thing…whatever that is."

"Well, the gala's coming up soon. Are you going?"

"I haven't decided. Besides, I don't have a date…yet. Listen, I can't talk. See you later." Sam hangs up on me. I can't believe it, because Sam is a lot of things but never rude to her friends.

"Albert, something is wrong with Sam."

"Well, honey, it *is* Sam." My sweet husband winks

and makes me melt even after all these years.

"I mean, something is amiss. You know how she gossips on the phone forever, especially about The Defenders. She didn't want to talk about anything, it seems."

"Nothing strange about that, honey. We're all getting older, you know. Maybe Samantha is running out of things to say … I hope."

"Albert, stop. She is my friend. I don't understand why she's been elusive since the reunion at the club. If it weren't for you…"

"If it weren't for me, what?" Albert drops his sketches on the table to face me.

"I don't know that I could handle this whole Char-Charles thing. I haven't even explained it to the kids yet."

"Too early—besides, making sense to the children is my parental job." Albert stands and pulls me close to him.

"I doubt parenting skills will ever come easy for me. I can't even parent myself, Albert. How do I handle that my sister is my brother, my best friend is slowly dying, Meghan trashed our friendship, and now Sam hangs up on me for the first time? What else is going to happen?"

"I don't know, babe, but I'm here for you whatever the future brings. Don't you know that by now?"

Chapter 22

Charles

"Anything interesting, my Defenders?"

"No, sir. Just that you are a mystery to family and their friends." Agnes, an employee of many years, reports flatly, unusual for her expressive Russian heritage.

"Yes, that's a given. Did Debbie understand where to deposit the check?"

"Sam explained too…ah, cryptically; she did not do a proficient job. I do not know if Debbie believes her."

I'm stunned. "Damn, that's unlike Sam. We need that money in the Caymans to begin our next phase."

"Son, I will attend the gala for you and verify the process to Debbie."

"No. Sam did her best, I'm sure. Debbie must know before the gala, anyway. I'll devise a different approach."

Uncharacteristically, Agnes grimaces but answers obediently. "Yes, sir."

"Keep up surveillance—I want to know if the Feds show up again, especially at Sam's."

I do a few projects on my own without notifying my staff. I require funds; firepower costs a lot, and I had overspent for the first time. Now, arms dealers threaten me. My legacy will not be destroyed because of inadequate finances; we have come too far. Maybe I should have waited on the human trafficking program. No, I will make this work. I learned to blend into the African jungles. Could I meld into a manicured estate?

"Where is Debbie on Monday nights?"

Agnes reviews surveillance records. "Always at home—too sick to teach."

Debbie had looked rough—a bone with lots of makeup. *She better last long enough to throw this gala.* "Bring up a 360-degree view of her residence."

Her Oyster Bay estate lay by the water—one of the many channels of the St. Mary's River that winds its way around the west side of Amelia, then inland south to Jacksonville and north to Georgia. Alligators, stingrays, porpoises, and sharks frequent those waterways.

"All right, perfect."

"Son?"

Our cramped quarters make privacy difficult, but a skeleton crew is barely affordable. Agnes volunteers her professional expertise for food and quarters. Donations bought the surveillance equipment that keeps me out of jail or worse.

"What phase is the moon?"

"Growing. Full tomorrow night."

Not safe; a die-hard fisherman or shrimper might spot me on the water. "Weather?"

"Much cloud cover, rain at forty percent."

That will do. "Agnes, I'm famished; you must be too. I'm using the office, so take a break."

"Yes, Charles. I bring you something to eat?" She sounds so Russian when she acts motherly.

"You know I eat rations, Agnes."

"Yes, but I see you losing much weight these last

149

few weeks. I worry about your health."

Always the mother, Agnes, and that's why you are here—a perfect profile for The Defenders.

"I appreciate your concern. Sure, bring something vegetarian with lots of protein." I will need it.

My volunteers are devoted to me and the cause. They endure intense screening before I accept them into the organization. Then, they train for months to learn defensive skills. When proficient in that skill, they learn guerrilla tactics, which are essential to protecting the animals. Only the best graduate to a vindicator level— removing poachers and their financial sources on and off the animal preservations.

To understand everyone's job, each Defender steps into various positions until they find their niche— intelligence, defensive field operations, surveillance, communications, procurement, and animal husbandry; the job descriptions continue.

All Defenders drop their birth names and walk the line between legal and illegal for the good of the cause. All receive a payment equal to the positions they secure, even if they receive only food rations and essential education for their entire family.

Participants remain inconspicuous to avoid retribution from poachers and business leaders who dictate animal killing for profit. Since law enforcement also wants to detain us, we protect our members from a double-edged sword. So far, most officials have ignored our actions.

Eventually, everyone finds their spot, but only a few aspire to or qualify for the offensive rank of vindicators. Vindicator status requires the sacrifice of family structure and social relations, as their lives most often reward them with safe houses, rations, and broken ties if captured or killed. They understand their families will quietly elevate to achieve higher education while enjoying wholesome food. All participants vow to protect Earth's creatures and each other unto death.

To fill skilled administrative positions, I had hired from the outside. Carson escaped from an assassin in Brazil after he hacked through a government site and proved corruption existed at the highest level. A former priest, Carson, resembles the man in Columbian Coffee ads without the burro. I count on his core altruism and obsession for life in all forms except evil. He believes in "removing" poachers as "the law is useless protecting the creatures made by God."

Carson only asks for room and board as he thinks money is the root of all evil. I provide anything he requires. Computer and engineering skills allow Carson to learn anything The Defenders require for a task. He learns how to make and use it, but most of all, how to get away with it if using explosives. Yet, he is a gentle soul who eats vegetarian, listens to classical music, and meditates daily. Yet, he can kill poachers without remorse like my other trusted employee, Agnes.

Agnes, a fiftyish widow with no living children or relatives, shows a keen ability to organize and manage. She had traveled from Yugoslavia to answer an ad I placed, elusive and puzzle-like. The test required someone to figure out where I hid the application for the job online. She was the only one to find it.

Then, Agnes answered every question about poaching with the same answer. "End it permanently by any means." The woman resembles a large-boned gypsy with wild, black hair, a streak of white running through the middle of it like a skunk. I half-suspect she can gaze into a crystal ball and tell the future.

After the murder of her son, considered an anarchist by the KGB, she fled Russia, but not before she poisoned those responsible for her son's death. She is proud of that fact to this day.

The elusive KGB, or what's left of it, would love to find Agnes, as she holds essential secrets that can expose past atrocities and implicate the current leader. Since her safe house in Yugoslavia has been compromised, Africa provides a perfect environment for her to disappear.

Agnes has been hyper vigilant with me since she failed to safeguard her only son. Although her psychology is slightly "off," her KGB training with computers and surveillance techniques balances the whole person. The days that she confuses me with her son are an acceptable risk. It is a powerful bond that I use to further my anti-poaching agenda.

Agnes safeguards all The Defenders, but mostly me. Both Carson and Agnes often travel with me, insulating me from harm. They will be prominent in future strategies, like utilizing The Defenders program for human trafficking.

For more complicated plots, like my solitary offensive—accessing Debbie's estate and house while it is under FBI surveillance—I need alone time to visualize. This plan requires even more finesse than usual since I must speak to Debbie directly.

When Agnes returns to the office, the precise time frames needed to accomplish this feat should be ready. Communication between my new crew is essential for this scheme to be foolproof. I trust that Agnes and Carson have chosen and train the first group of American

Defenders as well as they did in South Africa. They only had weeks to learn the basics for an operation.

After lunch, I inform Agnes and Carson of every nuance of my plan. The crew is more excited than I expected. But it is The Defender's first operation in the USA.

"My new family, American Defenders, I will leave you in Agnes and Carson's capable hands. These two individuals manage clandestine operations—listen to them."

I leave with a round of "Yes, sirs" from the team. I'm feeling confident. American Defenders treat me like a rock star.

Chapter 23

Homeland Defense

The plush office of the Department of Homeland Defense overlooks Washington, D.C., and includes a view of the capital. The secretary of Homeland Defense is in the middle of a lecture, banging her hand on her desk for emphasis.

"I don't give a flying fuck how beneficial everyone thinks he is. Innocenti is a damn murderer and an intruder in this country. I refuse to allow him to wreak havoc with his lopsided ideology in the USA. Find him before the FBI does. It's time we cage him like the animal he is."

"Yes, ma'am." The agents respond in unison.

The two agents travel down the elevator in complete silence. They enter the garage, nodding to fellow agents. Once they are inside the car, they relax.

"Madame Secretary should choose her words more carefully, Bob. The Defenders' whole purpose is to save endangered species and take out poachers while doing it. If Innocenti heads that organization, and that hasn't been proven yet, he does the world a favor."

"I agree, but this is the States, not Africa, India, or the Far East. No one will turn their heads here. If it isn't by the book or law, one can expect to go down in our country. That doesn't mean we prioritize Charles, though," Agent Robert Kinnear smiles.

"The workload is extensive," Agent Barkley notes.

"True. The FBI has stats on Charles …I'll start with them, but you know how slowly they share information."

"Let's hope so. I'll contact the local police force."

Barkley laughs. "That will take forever. Meanwhile, we can spend time on the real threats against our country and not animal-rights activists."

"Exactly. Our bosses roll in and out of here so quickly; nobody knows what is occurring anymore."

They enjoy a hearty laugh.

****

Charles

I put the Kayak into the water at sunset, estimating an hour to paddle to Debbie's estate. The full moon doesn't penetrate the cloud coverage as my camouflaged Kayak slices through choppy waters undetected. As planned, the last of the incoming tide helps quicken the trip—it is better to be too early than too late. It would be dead tide by the time I reach the estate.

Replica shorebirds anchored by my crew show the way. They lead to the final inlet with access to Debbie's dock. But that entry is too open and vulnerable. I round the bend, rowing toward the flooded marsh teeming with gators this night.

A dolphin pod surfaces as I paddle through the last stretch of deep water. Stingrays fly to make way, and marsh hens cackle a warning. A moment of pure pleasure invades my steely thoughts as I navigate the tricky ins and outs of the marsh. Without the full moon, the marsh grasses would be arid and unnavigable. I'd have to slosh my way through on foot. But with this moon phase, the marsh floods deep enough, so I paddle right to the bulkhead on the darker side of her grounds.

Fate supports me once again when I see that live oaks, oleanders, and Pampas grass growing in her backyard will provide coverage. After anchoring the kayak to the marsh floor, I smear myself with black mud and slip over the bulkhead.

The beady eyes of an alligator zero in on me. I lay flat on my belly, checking for any additional monitors since my crew inspected the grounds. Nothing has changed.

Crawling toward the grandeur of Debbie's home, I'm like a fiddler crab—small, unseen, and undetectable but checking forward and behind me. Although alligators aren't as predatory or vicious as crocs, they will attack easy prey. The bulkhead offers no protection from a hungry gator, as they climb easily.

Listening intensely for movement, I hear squeaky ow-ow sounds—baby gators. A protective momma must be close—too close.

****

Johnathan Johnson- actor

Johnathan Johnson hasn't worked in a month. Although sober for over six weeks, his drinking, blatant womanizing, and dramatic tantrums dried up his usual source of income from acting in local commercials and county theater.

An early morning phone call surprises him.

"Johnathan Johnson?"

"Yes, that's me." He speaks in his most resounding television voice.

"This is the Barras Agency. We are holding auditions for a movie and came across your resume. You look perfect for the part. You are six-foot, coal-black hair, muscular, yes?"

"Oh, yes, that's me. The type women want, and the man men want to be."

Agnes scowls but remembers to curb her Russian accent with American expressions. "Cool, Johnathan. Our audition is atypical of what you have experienced, as we don't use cattle calls. We would like to see you in a real-life scenario from the movie we are shooting.

"Even though you fit the lead's appearance exactly, we need to see you in action to be sure you can move well. Are you willing?"

"Yes, of course. Just tell me when and where; I'll be there."

The lead! Thank God I stopped drinking and lost some weight.

"We love cooperation, Johnathan. I will tell you the particulars if you have a pen and paper."

****

Sam

—*Are you home?*—

The text I get looks suspicious. Charles wouldn't text; he isn't stupid. Should I answer it? Maybe he is in trouble, or maybe he needs me? Okay, I'll play along and send a return text.

—*Yes. Monday always leaves me tired after the weekend. I am just sitting here.*—

—*Soon*—.

This is too cryptic. Charles wouldn't chance it, would he? No, he won't risk coming here because he knows the law watches my house.

Hmm. Now, I get it —those fuckers. The FBI will try to expose me as his accomplice or something worse.

What are they planning? There is only one way to find out.

After a quick shower, I slip into a new negligee. I set two wine glasses on a tray, along with cheese and fruit. I'm giddy before I open the wine, enjoying the ruse. Those FBI idiots have something planned, but two can play this game.

Let them think I am expecting someone special to arrive. Anyway, many people always text me, and I text back.

I situate the tray on the coffee table in the living room and choose an erotic movie, one with a heterosexual theme. Let officials think a man is coming to see me. I relax, sipping wine, smiling like the Cheshire Cat.

****

FBI

"Ms. Yu received communication, sir. The text says she's expecting company. Special guest, I suspect."

"Male or female? She rolls, either way, you know."

"Yes, sir. I expect a male visitor from what she is watching on TV."

"Have agents surround the house. By the time Charles enters, we will have him. Take him alive unless he is packing."

"Sir? He accomplished a great deal of good. He deserves fair treatment, Sir."

"Just give the order," Assistant Director barks.

"Yes, sir. Right now, sir…"

****

Charles

The crew dims the outside lights—tricky business without turning off everything simultaneously. That's the skill set I require. That allows one minute to reach the house before the lights turn back on.

Suddenly, I hear a growl behind me. Glowing eyes sit five feet away. I tear open the plastic bag that hangs around my neck and pitch the raw chicken parts over the gator's head. As she turns toward it, I run to the back wall trellis with no time to spare.

****

FBI

"There's a ruckus over at the estate, sir."

"Eyes on it now."

A silent drone lifts and shines a light on the source of the noise. "There it is, sir. Two gators are battling it out. Damn, I thought we had him for a second."

"No, not Charles. I assure you, he won't make a sound. Keep that drone at the ready, though."

****

Charles

Damn, drone. The team can't ground it, or it will sound an alarm.

My grappling hook, covered with a thick, pliable, rubber-like material, quietly grabs Debbie's balcony. It's a simple but effective tool. As I shimmy upward, a beeping alarm sounds in the front of the house—perfect timing.

****

FBI

"What the hell is that?"

"A smoke detector in the kitchen, sir."

"Fire?"

"No, sir, the alarm sounds when the battery needs changing. That is what the husband is cursing about. He is changing it, sir."

159

"The status of Sam's house?"

"Nothing yet, sir."

"How about Blair's?"

"No action whatsoever except for Blair singing lullabies…those poor kids."

"And Albert?"

"Painting in the studio, sir, as usual. The only action we might see is at Samantha's house."

"Let's hope so…"

"Wait, sir—Miss Yu's Street. A car parks nearby, dimming its lights."

"Where?"

"…about four blocks west from Samantha Yu's."

"Sir, a large figure is traveling through backyards, around houses. It appears he is zig-zagging but headed in Sam's direction."

Assistant Deputy Director whispers, "Ha. No jungle to hide in —new territory for him. Wait until he gets inside, then arrest him. I want Sam for aiding and abetting, too."

"Hold until he is inside. Repeat, hold until he is inside."

****

Sam

Two hours pass, but all I have is time. I select another movie when I hear a tap on my bedroom door. Oh my God, Charles is here. Is he crazy? Should I answer it? I can't ignore it. My heart pounds as I unlock the sliders and open the door just enough to let him slip through.

"Aiya. What is this?" I'm baffled.

"Has it been so long that you don't recognize me, darling?" He winks.

I'm not sure what to say. Did Charles send him? Suddenly, men throw open the slider.

"Get down on the floor. Put your hands behind your back."

The stranger does as directed but snarls. "You agents will regret this."

Before the agent's handcuffs can immobilize him, the stranger flashes a small revolver. Shots fire in my bedroom as I dive under the bed shrieking … then, nothing but silence and the sound of my breathing. It's over as fast as it begins.

"Ms. Yu. Back out from under the bed slowly. Hands up, now."

I push my quivering body out and try to stand, but my legs shake so much that I fall to the floor, where I get a good look at my intruder's face; he is shot to smithereens, his face a bloody pulp.

I cry hysterically; I can't even swear. *That could have been my love, my Charles. It could have been me.*

An agent yanks me up, forces my arms around my back, and cuffs me, showing no mercy like I'm a typical hood.

"You saw him pull the gun, didn't you?" the agent asks but seems to tell me, too, insistently.

I can only nod my head up and down.

"Sir?" Another agent attempts to get his superior's attention.

"Quiet. Read Miss Yu her rights and load her up."

"Sir?"

"Search the place for evidence, and…"

"*Sir?*"

"What the hell is it?" The boss is riding high for his capture.

"The perpetrator's gun, sir," the agent says softly.

"What about it?"

"It isn't real, sir."

"What do you mean it isn't real, agent?"

"It's fake, sir—rubber or something like it."

The agent picks up the weapon with gloved hands and brings it to his boss.

"You must be kidding."

"No, sir. Charles used a phony gun."

"You mother fuckers, you killed an unarmed man. Aiya. You almost killed me, too. You sick mother fuckers; you sick." I shout hysterically.

"Get her out of here. It must be an intended suicide by authorities, but why? Fuck. Now, we'll have The Defenders' supporters wanting to hang my ass... I mean our asses."

Chapter 24

Debbie

"Greg, I'm going to bed."

"Okay, darlin, I have a few more pages to edit, then I'll join you."

I am breathless when I reach the top of the stairs. I lean on the wall until I catch my breath. Then, I saunter into the bedroom, realizing my energy escaped earlier than usual. "Damn liver."

As I step into the bathroom, I'm startled by a whisper in my ear.

"Debbie, it's Charles. Don't turn on the light. Open the faucet and whisper."

I'm too tired to be shocked and let the water run full force.

"Before you curse me out, know we're both under surveillance. Listen carefully. Offer the donors a deal. The one who transfers the most cash directly into the Defenders 501 K, the Cayman Islands account in the next few days will win a prize."

So, Sam did hear that information. I nod silently, wishing he'd talk to my face instead of from behind.

"Come up with an appealing gift for them. The government may soon stop the banks from cashing donation checks in the U. S.—anything to flush me out. So make sure money is deposited directly into the

Cayman 501k. I need that cash to implement the child trafficking program. Can you fix it, Debbie?"

"Of course, I can. I'll work on a plan tonight. The gala is a week away, so don't expect miracles. But I'm already thinking of something. We could award safaris to a few African preserves for the winning donor. How does that sound? Charles?"

I cringe, hoping I wasn't too loud with his name. I turn off the faucet and walk through the bathroom outside to the darkness of the balcony, but I see no one. Charles has melted into the night like I imagine he does in the jungles.

"Hey, what are you doing standing in the dark?" Albert asks.

"Thinking about the gala. I'll stay up longer and ensure I got everything right." I place my finger over my lips in a sh. "We're bugged," I whisper in his ear. "Go to bed, handsome; I'll tell you about it in the morning."

Greg returns the whisper, "They bugged our house? The whole house?" I nod, and Greg plays the part perfectly.

"Yeah, well, I knew you wouldn't be in the mood if I took too long. But I am exhausted. I'll be asleep in a minute anyway." Greg winks and pats my butt.

"Thanks. I'll be sure not to wake you when I come to bed."

I'm amazed at the man who stands by my side and loves me through a catastrophic health crisis. I'm not the sexy dish he married, but I do my best to keep looking presentable… in case I live and in case I don't. I want my man to remember me with a smile.

Once I'm in my study, I devise a solution to quicken the incoming donations. The update about the gala reads.

BE OUR GALA WINNER

Transferring funds directly into The Defenders 501k Cayman Island account in the next three days qualifies you to win:

PRIZES

*Highest donation wins a safari for four.

*Second highest donation wins a safari for two.

Let's save the trafficked children. Let's defend The Defenders!

Attendance is not required but is appreciated. *Remember, all donations are tax-deductible!*

I send the notice to everyone invited to the gala, wishing I had thought of this idea earlier. There was a time when no one would have had to remind me of anything. My mind is melting like a candle, its wick floating in the wax.

****

FBI

"I want this body identified immediately, Coroner," Assistant Deputy Director orders.

"Your men didn't make it easy. They blasted his dentistry to smithereens, but I'll do my best."

The irritated coroner strides beside the rolling gurney to the ambulance.

"I'll meet you at the morgue, boys. Don't lose this one—mighty important."

"Do we ever?" The driver looks offended.

"Just get it there safe and fast."

Damn FBI bullies. Now I'm turning into a hard ass, too.

****

Sam

A security officer escorts me to the assistant deputy

director's office. At least this agent treats me gently, but I'm still handcuffed with a blanket draped around me; my negligee brought too many stares.

My eyes burn red and are swollen, my nose is clogged, and the cuffs bite into my wrists. "I want to call my lawyer."

My voice seems weak, like when a geriatric person speaks. I've aged decades in minutes.

"Sure, in a second. But Ms. Yu, you got a good look at the man you let into your house. We want you to verify it was Charles Innocenti."

The assistant deputy director barks at me. I stop sniveling. "What?"

"My men know him from a few obscure photos of Charlotte. Only you can tell us if we shot the right fellow."

My brain races, and my strength rises. "You shot at a man you couldn't verify as Charles? But you shot anyway? What kind of monsters are you?"

Assistant Deputy asshole leans over the desk into my face. "That turnaround won't work on me, ma'am. I want the truth now. Was that Charles?"

"It was dark in my room; it sounded like him, so I let him in. I wouldn't let in a stranger! But before I turn on the light, you burst into my house with guns drawn and shoot, and now you want my cooperation? Well, put me in jail. When my lawyer arrives, I'll give you all the information you want."

"But you did verify that it was him, Ms. Yu. You 'wouldn't let a stranger in,' you said."

I pull my wrists apart so the cuffs hurt even more, making it easier to break into a howl, waterworks and all. I place my head on the desk, hoping to hide the smile that is trying to break free. *Charles is safe, and they don't even know it.*

My drama irritates the assistant deputy jerk. "Take the cuffs off. Let Ms. Yu make a call, and then place her in holding."

I pretend to be weak, so the kind agent gives me a minute to collect myself while the assistant deputy dummy picks up the phone.

"Director? We got him. Yes, sir. He pulled a weapon, so my men took him down."

"Yes, his body is at the coroner's as we speak, waiting for identification, but the girlfriend admitted it was him.

"Calling Homeland Security? I don't envy you that job, sir. They wanted this collar. Yes, sir. Good luck. What's that, sir?

"Yes, I'll keep it out of the press if that's what you want…well, yes, I realize how popular Charles is or was, but my men shot in self-defense. Ah, sir, I said we'll keep it out of the press. Yes, sir. It's as good as done.

"Agent," I said, "get her out of here."

"Yes, sir. She seemed dizzy and weak upon standing—just giving her a moment, sir."

"Carry her if you have to."

"Yes, sir."

"No, I'm fine now. I needed a moment to catch my breath." As I leave, I hear the diminutive assistant dunce mumble.

"Damned if I do. Damned if I don't."

Aiya. That's right.

****

"Debbie, it's Sam. The fucking FBI has me; I need an attorney and bail. They're accusing me of cooperating

167

with Charles tonight, harboring a fugitive, anything they can think of to keep me locked up like a wild animal."

"Hm. That doesn't sound right or lawful. They are in the wrong here."

"They shot...Charles ... an hour ago. I'll explain when you get here." I whisper as though an FBI bug couldn't hear it.

"What? I'll send Albert with an attorney right now. We need to talk."

"Come too, if you can, please! But don't call Blair tonight—let her sleep."

"Oh, I won't, Sam. Don't worry about that, darlin'. We won't tell her any news until tomorrow, okay?"

"Good. I need a friend here; please hurry."

"Sam, I'll be there before you can say defender a hundred times. Relax until then."

"Thanks, Debbie. I'll try, but I don't know what these morons have next on their agenda."

****

FBI vs. Coroner

"Did you record the phone conversation?" Assistant Deputy Director asks.

"Yes, sir, although I wouldn't say the surveillance was legal...sir." The lower-level agent cringes, irked to do something against a citizen's rights again.

"I don't want to hear that out of your mouth, agent. Was anything suspicious said? I want Ms. Yu and Mrs. Duke charged with aiding and abetting too."

"Mrs. Duke? Ah, no, sir. Nothing seems out of place at all. Ms. Yu asked for an attorney and bail only."

"What about Innocenti's sister?"

"They plan to break the news of his death to her in the morning."

The Assistant Director snickers. "Well, that's mighty nice of them."

The agent agrees. "Yes, sir. Why wake up someone to tell them their brother is dead? That would be cruel."

"Would it now? Get Blair Finney on the line for me."

"Sir?" The agent shakes his head in disbelief.

"I want to hear her reaction first-hand...now, agent!"

"Yes, sir." The agent reluctantly calls for his boss.

"I bet every one of those women is aiding Charles."

On the third ring, Blair answers.

"Blair Finney?"

"Yes, this is Mrs. Finney. Do you know how late it is? Who is this?"

"I'm FBI Assistant Deputy Director—"

"FBI? The FBI calls in the middle of the night? It better be important. My family needs a full night's sleep."

"It is important. It's about your brother."

"Charles? Isn't he back in Africa by now? Oh, God, what's happened to him?"

"Charles pulled a gun on my men tonight. We shot him; he's dead."

"What? My brother...my Char is dead?" The cell makes a loud noise when it hits the floor, followed by another thud. The director hears footsteps and hollering.

"Who the hell is this, and what have you said to my wife?" Albert says.

"FBI, sir. I relayed the news about Charles to your wife. He's dead. Is she not handling it well?"

"Not handling it? She's out cold. I swear to God, if I can't wake her, I'll have your head on a stake and everything else that is dear to you."

"Ah, Mr. Finney, we have the right to…hello, hello? The bastard hung up. Well, I guess that call told me what I wanted to know. Lucky for that family, Innocenti's sister is clueless. Get me the coroner."

"Yes, sir."

****

Coroner

"What? It's midnight for Christ's sake, and I told you that your men blasted his teeth to bits. I can't pull up dental records as usual. It could be at least a week before I verify the remaining molars. FBI or no FBI, don't you fucking holler at me or call me at home in the middle of the night. Teach your men how to kill without blowing up the target's face, for Christ's sake."

I hang up, pleased that I didn't share that the fingerprints don't match Char Innocenti's.

"Well, that asshole didn't ask about the prints. Damned if I'm going to tell him something he didn't require of me. I'll call Homeland Security first thing in the morning. Someone with brains needs to know what's going on."

****

FBI

The assistant deputy director yawns. "I need to sleep. The rest of you might as well get rest, too. We'll start back at seven. Don't be late."

"Sir, it's midnight. We haven't had a decent night's sleep in days."

"You understand the importance of stopping Innocenti before he begins killing in this country. Seven a.m. prompt."

"Yes, sir."

****

Charles

The return trip from Debbie's estate is uneventful until I reach the inlet of Eagan's Creek. I navigate around sandbars that have ruined many boats of inexperienced sailors. Unfortunately, the clouds have disappeared, and the moon shines down on me like a stage light. There is no hiding.

A low, yellow light shines across the water up ahead. I suspect company may be waiting for me near the boat ramp. As I row closer, I see someone in a uniform standing by a car with his flashlight.

"Halt. Who goes there?"

"Just giggin' for flounder. Who are you?" I shout in my most southern accent.

"Homeland Security. You're fishing in a Kayak? In the middle of the night?"

"Yes, sir. But I tipped, lost my gig, and all the flounder I caught. It hasn't been a good night."

"Tie up. Get out of the boat slowly, hands up."

"What, for giggin' at night?"

"Just do it."

"Yes, sir. Tide is strong and hard coming back in; let me maneuver …"

"Watch out there; don't tip the boat. This creek is full of gators. Hey!" The guard panics when I gauge the water with my paddle and turn the kayak upside down.

"Help, help, I don't swim well. Please help," I holler as I surface, letting the tide carry me further away. Then, to be convincing, I gargle a bit of water.

"Shit, God damn." The guard must be unsure about his next move. He must be assessing if I'm worth risking his life in the running tide. I hope he doesn't. He's an

171

innocent man doing his job.

I pretend to swallow some more water and go under several times. If I need to, I can swim to one of the boats on the creek when I go under the last time.

Finally, he starts down the muddy boat ramp when the unthinkable happens. The fellow slips and falls backward, banging his head on the concrete. He doesn't get up, and he doesn't move.

I hurry before he regains consciousness. A nearby slew has captured my kayak, so I yank it out and use my knife to punch holes in the bottom of it. I pull it to the creek's center and release it to float with the outgoing tide, where it will finally submerge in the Intracoastal.

I pull myself onto a dock and slink away as the officer's truck runs with its headlights on and radio sounding. "Respond, please. Respond."

My crew had planted warm clothes for me. I change into them, but I can't leave an injured innocent. I search the area; the officer and I are still alone. Quickly, I shine a light on his face. His vacant eyes stare into the darkness, and blood trails down the ramp into the water. One crack of the head, and he's gone. There is nothing I can do for him. Nature will step in.

As planned, I signal a drone that kept watch for me. A driver meets me in a battered truck and drives me off the island's south end. Although I'm eager to return to my African jungles, a homeland security officer is down. I'll be a suspect for that, too; the law will order surveillance on every available mode of transportation.

I must find a different exit at a less dangerous time.

****

FBI

Assistant Deputy Director speaks stoically. Director

Robert S. Trainer gives him a minute to explain.

"Sir, agents cover all airports, bus, and train stations watching for Charles, anyone that looks like Charles. Both entrances and exits are under surveillance. He won't get away in this region, sir."

Director Trainer scowls at the Assistant Deputy. "Thanks to you, Homeland Security has taken the lead on this investigation. Too little, too late—you bungled this case from the beginning—shooting an innocent man, an actor no less, and arresting a woman who promises to be nothing but cooperative.

"Then you call an outstanding citizen in the middle of the night to tell her that her brother is dead. To top it off, you harass the coroner. It is time you go on vacation, a very long vacation. You are fired."

"Sir, I followed protocol. I am not responsible for an actor pulling a rubber gun."

"Oh, but you are…or should I say, were. Your weapon and badge…now."

Chapter 25

Debbie

Finally, my work has paid off. I'm thrilled at the turnout at the gala. The convention hall looks spectacular. Hiring a friend, an amusement park professional, was worth it to transform the entire building into an African preserve during the setting sun.

Thousands of twinkling stars from above light the room with enough luminescence to see the backdrops my crews have built. It's a miniature Africa with animated monkeys, lions, and elephants that sound intermittently. Discreetly in a corner are cages with child actors gagged and bound. It's a compelling reminder of The Defenders' past success and the hope for their future success against child traffickers.

It's time to begin the "Evening in Africa Masquerade Gala." Greg escorts me to the podium. My legs shake as though they may crumble beneath me.

"Ladies and gentlemen, I hope y'all enjoy your evening in Africa."

A round of applause arises as attendees admire their realistic and transporting surroundings. Many have chosen elephant and rhino masks or headdresses. I wear a simple chimpanzee eye mask.

"Many of our families have known each other for decades. It is marvelous how we stay in touch. We also welcome the new faces hidden among us—political, newly rich tech geeks, and Hollywood stars. We adopt you into our circle of benefactors who foster poignant causes that affect our society." A round of applause sounds.

"In the past, we've given generously to The Defenders, who risk their lives saving endangered species. I hope the venue around this room will help to remind you of their successes.

"The Defenders go where we cannot, and tonight's gala promotes The Defender's new program that takes them from jungles to cities, including our most beloved America. With our help, The Defenders begin a new quest: eradicating human trafficking from the face of this earth."

Another round of applause builds my strength to continue.

"I've sent you the photos and statistics. Stealing innocent children for this horrible trade is unacceptable. So, let's all be generous, as our United States has allowed this horror to enter and thrive within our borders. Yes, we've all heard of countries like Thailand, Portugal, and Brazil, where perverts pay large sums for the unthinkable. But here? In our blessed country?

"Are your children and their children safe on our streets? No, not anymore. We must change that by contributing to The Defenders, who will exterminate human traffickers in our country and beyond."

Applause greets me. I smile and nod despite having to hold on to the lectern to counter the weakness in my body.

"As you know, attendance is not required to win the safaris. However, a couple of supporters, who have donated generously, relinquished their rights to the prizes. They've already enjoyed safaris numerous times and hoped for others to experience the magnificence of Africa. I want to thank them.

"First, Bob and Melony Gatlin, thank you for donating five million dollars." A gasp arises, but I hold up my hand for quiet. "But Weston Bruce insisted on out-donating the Gatlin's with five million and one dollars."

Whoop, whistles, and applause resound. "I can't express The Defender's gratitude for these gifts. I warn all human traffickers: you can run, you can hide, but after tonight, you are on notice: The Defenders will eliminate you like the child poachers you are."

The crowd claps again. "Hear, hear" echoes.

"I thank each of you for your donations to this urgent call. We'll announce our Safari winners after dinner. Until then, enjoy the entertainment and the fine dining, and feel proud knowing you are a part of the solution. Ladies and gentlemen, dinner is served. Bon Appetit!"

Greg retrieves me from the stage, glued to my side, supporting my body. I'm grateful for the surge of adrenaline that answered every round of applause.

"You were wonderful, sweetheart."

I love making Greg proud.

Blair and Albert, wearing elephant ears and grey masks, hug me gently. "You are a wonder, Debbie. Look at this crowd, this room."

"Thank you. I'm pleased with the turnout. But where is Sam? Is she still too traumatized to attend?"

Before Blair answers me, I squint through the hazy African evening to see a stunning, model-type blonde wearing couture approaching with Sam's arm looped through hers. The blonde wears the full mask of a Cheetah while Sam dons a headdress with two tusks protruding from each side of her cheeks. The headdress doesn't detract from Sam's glow of happiness. Her designer gown complements the blonde's. Their sequins reflect the twinkling starlight from above.

"Victoria, meet my friends, Blair, Albert, Gregory, and his lovely wife, Debbie. I'd like y'all to meet my date, Victoria Walker."

"Hello, so very nice to meet you, Victoria."

"Please, call me Vicki. Likewise, I'm sure. Sam's told me so much about you, Debbie."

"Oh my, you sound like you're from Texas…?"

"You have a good ear."

"Vicky, I haven't seen Sam smile like this since… since."

Sam interjects quickly. "Those FBI agents shook me up. Thank you for coming to my rescue. I keep looking over my shoulder, expecting one to jump me, especially since I found another bug in my lamp this evening. What they hope to discover, I don't know."

"Shook you up?" Blair says. "I still have a knot on my head from when I hit the floor. Thank God Albert was home. He gave them what for."

I shake my head. "I don't understand that bunch. No wonder crime runs rampant."

"From what I hear, sweetheart, The Defenders don't have much to do with Charles anymore."

Greg is right. "I don't know why the law bothers him. Anyway, I heard he's disappeared."

"Now, that's a sad thing. But I certainly hope The Defenders carry the torch for him. Such a fine organization," Vicky says softly.

Sam sadly conveys the latest news. "Well, I hear they found a Homeland Security agent dead on Egan's creek or what's left of him. Gators chewed off his feet before officers arrived. They want to blame Charles for anything to have a reason for more surveillance."

"I hadn't heard that news."

"They've kept it under wraps, so the locals don't panic."

"Debbie, I'm so impressed with how you handled this gala. If ever I need advice with my Texas oilmen, may I contact you?"

"Sure. Sam has my number. It was more fun than trouble. Citizens love The Defenders; they are like modern-day superheroes. Influential people phoned to ask for invitations."

"How wonderful. I'm sorry we can't stay for the festivities, but I have a previous engagement. Sam insisted I peek in on the event before we continued, and I'm so glad I did. Until we meet again, Debbie, take care. I'm delighted to have met you all."

"You too, Vicky. I'm sorry you can't stay. Take good care of Sam."

"I'm persuading her to come away for a nice restful vacation."

Blair encourages them. "Well, Sam, that's a great idea, girlfriend. You could do with a rest, not more legalities."

Sam hooks her arm into Vicky's and nods, smiling peacefully as she says goodbye.

"Let's get you seated, Snacks." Greg takes good care of me.

"Somehow, you sat us in the middle of this throng

instead of at your table?" Blair peers at me sideways.

"I'm sorry. I must convince a few high rollers to give more. We'll get together after the event."

"I forgive you, then." She and Albert weave through the tables to their assigned seats.

"Come on, love, let me push that chair under the table for you."

"Greg, you are a worrywart, and I love you for it."

"Debbie." Meghan stands next to me in a business suit inappropriate for the occasion.

"Meghan, what are you doing here?"

Greg glares at her. "This is not the time."

"I can still defend myself, Sir Lancelot." I squeeze his dimpled chin between my thumb and finger. "Like Greg said, what are you doing here?"

"You win, Debbie—you, Blair, and Sam. You helped The Defenders into the next decades."

"Again, Meghan, why are you here?"

"To congratulate you—I came to let bygones be bygones."

"I am not quite as gracious as you think I am. You hurt Blair and Sam deeply, calling Charles a murderer then, calling the FBI on him."

"I stated the truth as I saw it at that time."

"Well, you were wrong." Greg is in Meghan's face as she nods.

"I saw Sam talking to you in the company of a rather tall blond."

"And? You know Sam swings both ways."

"That's right. Many people do these days, don't they? Listen, I came here beaten. I'm not going against Gatlin's or Bruce's because there's nothing but trouble for me. Finally, I see some things from their perspective.

I'm not saying I'm not conflicted, but it's a slow process adapting to another's viewpoint."

"Well…I'm thrilled you are trying. I wish you had thought of that earlier. As far as friendship is concerned, I'll leave that to Blair and Sam. They were the ones you hurt most by your allegations."

"Maybe Sam has softened toward me now that she has a new friend…what's her name again?"

"I never told you her name. I'll leave that to Sam. Now, I have work to do. Will you see yourself out? The Gala is by invitation only."

"Yes, of course. I am sorry, Debbie. I hope to see you soon."

Chapter 26

Charles

"Do you think we fooled them, Vicki?"

"Yes. The old Debbie would have caught on immediately. Sad what those transfusions are doing to her brain processes."

"Well, they keep her alive. I'm afraid she missed a few spots by the hairline, where I saw a yellow tinge. I can't stand the idea of losing her."

"Don't worry. I'm sure a liver will become available for her soon."

"Well, thanks for giving me a chance to say goodbye just in case." Sam grimaces. "Aiya. I'm taking off these platforms. It was nice being tall for a little while, but my feet are killing me."

"I'll have to massage them for you, but it was important to make me look shorter than I am. You standing next to me with those heels made me look closer to 5'8 or 9."

"That was a clever idea, Charles... I mean, Vicky."

"Don't worry, Sam; my crew checked the rental. It's bug-free." Sam peeks as I exchange my evening gown and girdle for a skirt with a matching long-sleeve, loose-fitting blouse. She catches her breath, trying to avert her eyes when noticing my pectoral and arm muscles. That surprises me; she's not like the uninhibited Sam I remember.

She slips into a sundress with sandals. The driver's seat inches forward as far as it will go, and Sam starts the car.

"Get comfortable. Mexico is a long drive from here." Sam is giddy as she heads down the highway toward I-10 West.

"I'll drive once you become too tired. I hope this disguise works as well as the couture did."

"Well, I'm not sure about fooling Albert; he has that artist's eye. But with that wig and facemask, you fooled your sister. I'm sorry you had to shave off the mustache, but you had no choice. You know, you turn me on no matter what sex you choose. It's like being in love with two people. I'll show you how much you excite me when we reach Mexico?"

I can only smile and nod in reply.

"You still use words sparingly?"

"I prefer action over words."

Sam's breath quickens, probably thinking ahead to alone time with me in a lovely hotel room. Before she continues the topic, I put in earbuds and close my eyes.

"Oh, if you can't keep me company, I'll chug one of these Awake drinks. They help when I stay up all night working on computer software, refining my skills—not that I need refining."

Finally, Sam clams up. She must understand that I don't want conversation. As I pretend to sleep, we spend the first part of the trip listening to an audible book on her phone—a spy thriller.

By morning, we pass Texan oil wells. I catnap on and off most of the way, saving my strength for the other side of the border.

****

Mexican Border

"Passports."

"Aiya. Sleepyhead, passports on the dashboard. My arms are too short." I quickly pass the documents to Sam.

"Here you go," she chirps to the guard. The Border Patrol examines the passports, carefully matching them to the driver's license photos.

"Reason for visiting Mexico?"

"A long-needed vacation," Sam says truthfully.

The agent returns the passports, and we cross the border.

"Charles, we made it. We are in Mexico. Arriba!"

Spanish sounds strange combined with a Chinese accent.

"Where do we stop? After driving twenty-five hours, I need to rest."

"You should. I'll drive from here, and you get shut-eye. I'll wake you when we arrive at the hotel."

Sam pulls over, and we exchange places. She lays the seat back and curls into a ball like a young cheetah. A couple of miles down the road, she begins to snuffle. It has worsened since our African adventure. Now, she sounds like a baby elephant trumpeting.

An hour later, I reach into my pocket, pulling out a baggie with a cloth inside. While driving, I open it and hold it under Sam's nose, letting her breathe it deeply. "This will stop the infernal snorts and help you stay asleep longer, little one."

A dumpy roadside motel appears ahead. I slow the car, pulling into its dusty, pot-holed drive. As expected, Sam remains asleep even over the ruts and bumps. A jeep pulls next to us, spewing up dust that reminds me of the dry season in Africa. I take a last look at Sam, and something tugs at me. Odd—I'm not prone to sentimentalities.

I grab my passport and exchange places with the Jeep's driver, leaving the rented SUV behind me. Heading south, I watch in the rearview as the rental crosses the road, traveling back north with its sleeping passenger.

****

Sam

"That was a good rest. Hey, where are you, Charles? Where are we? This sure isn't a luxurious hotel. A dirty trailer is the only thing I see."

"Charles?"

Maybe he had to use the toilet. I see a small airfield across from the parking lot. What the hell? A yawn overcomes me. I'm still exhausted. But what is this? An envelope sits on the dashboard in front of me. Even before I open it, I shake, sensing something horrible. I don't want to open it, but I force myself.

Dearest Sam:

I'm sorry to leave you this way. Plans changed. I don't want to implicate you anymore or put you in danger while on the run. Use the ticket to take a private plane home. Don't worry about the rental; a defender will return it. I know you are disappointed, but remember, I owe you a foot massage and so much more. I am heading into South America with you in my heart. Always Yours,

Charles

"Aiya!" I beat the dashboard until the pain becomes too much for my fists. I crumple in a fit of tears—twenty years' worth. Finally, I pull myself together. *Nobody treats me this way and gets away with it.*

When I open the door, nothing but stinking hot air greets me. Sweat soaks my face as I try to make sense of where I am. Finally, I pull my bag out of the trunk and wheel it into a small trailer used as an office. My body won't move normally; I feel so weak.

The one employee behind the desk takes my ticket without a hello.

"Oh, Ms. Yu. You rented a private plane to fly you over the border. We've been waiting. You are quite late."

"Yeah, well, I slept too long, okay? I'll use the restroom. Just take my bag. Then, point me toward the plane, please."

After peeing forever, I shuffle to a filthy sink and wipe off every bit of makeup that reminds me of my happiness during the gala. I squeeze a soaked paper towel on the back of my neck. It wakes me up and eases the unusual sluggishness all over my body. I better call the girls. I reach for my phone inside my pocket where I usually keep it. But it is gone. Nothing is in my purse. Maybe I left it in the car?

Running to the parking lot, I find the car has disappeared. Now, I'm out of breath from the heat. No. This feels worse than the heat.

At least the trailer has air conditioning. A man hurries toward me, and I can't help but whine at him. "She drugged me; that's why I feel so awful. And there is no way to text the girls. Maybe I packed the phone in my bag by mistake."

"Ms. Yu, I stored the luggage. I have a schedule that is already running behind." He sounds like a military officer.

"Yeah, okay. Nobody knows where I am or what I'm doing."

"Don't worry; I filed a flight plan that includes your name."

I follow him to a tiny plane, no longer caring about the damn phone. "Aiya. Too little. Too little. Your plane scares me."

"It won't be a long flight," the pilot says gently.

"It still scares me." My knees knock. "I don't want to get on it."

"Miss Yu, my thirty years plus experience should instill some confidence and make you feel better."

"Yeah, okay. But what is your fail-safe?"

"My fail-safe?"

He looks amused, but I'm too tired to care. "Yeah. You have one of those seats that send you up with a button; you know, it has a parachute on it and …"

"No, Miss Yu, there are no ejection seats."

"I'm not getting in."

The pilot takes a few seconds to find a solution. "Would you feel safer if you wore a parachute?"

I don't know if he is joking or not. "That wind-up toy needs a parachute…but, okay. I like something." My head hurts. I'm nauseated. I feel weirdly limp. I desperately want to be home with my real friends.

"Well, this is a first, but you won't need it."

"I'll take it anyway." I'm doing my best to hold my temper as I wrestle with my body's strange heaviness, as though my legs gained twenty pounds each. I can't think, either. The pilot jogs to the office and returns with one parachute.

"Where's yours?"

"I won't need it, I'm sure." The pilot smirks at me,

but I'm too depressed to care.

"Okay, can you help me put this on?"

The pilot tightens the final strap. "No more delays, Miss Yu. I want to be home before dark. I have a new grandbaby to meet. Let's go."

"Sure. Okay." Reluctantly, I climb in and buckle up.

"Do you know how to use a parachute, Miss Yu?"

"Know how? I pull this thing, I suppose. I better figure it out before I hit the ground."

The pilot laughs and starts the plane down the runway. "I can't wait to tell my wife about you, Miss Yu. But, yes, you pull that thing."

I ignore his comments. I have cottonmouth, and my head is too dull to lose my temper. "Hey, where are you flying me?"

"San Antonio, ma'am. You can take a flight from there to wherever you want."

"Yeah. Better than driving again." *Damn Innocenti.* My heartbreak penetrates my soul. The pilot notices a tear trailing down my cheekbone before I can wipe it away.

"Ma'am. Anything I can do? You don't look happy."

"I don't want to talk about my broken heart."

"I'm sorry, ma'am." At least the pilot shows some compassion, but my emotions begin to win.

"Not as sorry as I am for being such a stupid, fucking, idiotic fool!" I rage as the plane reaches altitude. As the last of my pent-up anger releases, I hear BOOM!

Chapter 27

Blair

A dream-like worry inside my sleeping brain wakes me. I can't determine what it is, but it weighs on me like a heaviness in my heart. Still, duty calls. I scramble out of bed, prepare the children for school, pack their lunches, and wake up Albert by whispering in his ear. "It's time, Daddy-O."

I've finished my mommy chores; now it's daddy's job to drive the children to school. That way, I can prepare for the day's work. "Bye, Charlotte. Bye, Buddy. Love you. Learn a lot today." I say the same thing every day.

"Love you, Mommy." Buddy is the first to say goodbye but is still reluctant to go to kindergarten. He is Albert's and my surprise child and the proverbial momma's boy. I confess that I love being a mom.

But being pregnant with Buddy in my forties terrified me. I begged for a C-section. Buddy must have heard me in the womb as his head stuck in my rib cage; he was unable to turn in the head-down position. The doctor operated to deliver a healthy eight-pound, seven-ounce boy.

"Later, Mom." Charlotte is five years older, acting too independent for her age. Albert and I planned her birth and conceived after a few months of trying. But contractions came on suddenly. By the time I got to the hospital, it was too late to give me medication of any kind. Charlotte was in the birth canal but was breech. I endured twenty-eight hours of labor, swearing I'd never be pregnant again.

"One is enough, Albert." Famous last words.

"Be home soon, sugar. Let's go, kids." Albert handles the children with ease. They adore him. How did I get so lucky? How could I be so blessed? Still, something feels wrong. Last night's dream about Sam won't let go. Although I don't remember it completely, I recall Sam crying out for help before I woke up sweating. I'll call Debbie.

"Good morning, my amazing friend. I don't suppose you've heard from Sam lately?"

"No. The last time I saw her, she was at the gala but going off on vacation with the woman we met. I hope she's having a good time."

"Deb, your voice sounds a little puny."

"I'm tired, that's all. Bad livers are such a bother. Blair?"

"Yes?"

"I'm glad you stopped drinking. Teach your kids not to drink, okay?"

"I've already begun programming them against alcohol. It's not just you—my mom, you know. They must be careful. We need to get together. I haven't seen you since the gala, and that was a week ago."

"Sure, as soon as I feel better, okay?"

"Of course. A match for your liver will come at any time now. I feel it."

"Yes, well, A-negative blood type isn't that common."

"Maybe not, but...I love you. I can't wait until you're back in good form again."

"We had some good laughs and tears, didn't we?"

"And we'll have more to come; just you wait and see."

"Sure, we will. In the meantime, think about forgiving Meghan, all right? Talk to Sam about it."

"Your heart is bigger than mine, but I'll consider it. I won't promise anything, though."

"That's all I ask. Greg's out shopping, so I'll crawl under the covers to snooze."

"Well, then, I'll let you go. Sweet dreams and all that."

My best friend is at death's door, and there isn't a thing I can do about it. I spend the rest of the morning at my home office with thoughts of Meghan and Sam interrupting my concentration. Later, Albert brings a salad, and we enjoy a brief lunch together but jump back to work, knowing parental duties begin again mid-afternoon.

Just as I finish my projects for the day, I hear the front door open.

"Mommy, Buddy hit a kid who was making fun of me. He's in big trouble at school." I greet them in the foyer.

"Buddy, is that true?"

"He made fun of Charlotte's snaggletooth, Mommy."

"First of all, Buddy, I never want you to hit anyone. Use your brain, not your brawn."

"Yes, ma'am."

Buddy has the cutest pout. "Secondly, I'm proud of you for wanting to protect Charlotte."

Buddy grins at his big sister, Charles's namesake, who would need braces sooner rather than later.

"So, what do you do next time?"

"Tell him he's stupid and wait for him to try and hit me first?"

"Albert, I need you."

"I'm here." Albert stands in the hallway, arms crossed, amused after hearing the entire conversation. "Having a problem conveying your thoughts, sweetie?"

"Something like that. Kids, head on down to Dad's studio. His fridge has new after-school snacks. It's daddy time while I figure out where your Auntie Sam went. By the way, Albert, have you spoken to Greg lately?"

"No. Why?"

"Debbie sounds weaker than usual."

"She is weak and very sick, sweetheart. I told you to prepare yourself."

"I can't. I won't go down that road. Just go on. The kids are waiting for a talk about fighting. And Albert?"

"That's my name."

"Thank you for being everything I can't be for the kids."

"Don't be so hard on yourself. You've come a long, long way with them, and I love you for it."

I am, without a doubt, the luckiest woman in the world. Albert understands my lack of upbringing, which includes a lack of motherly affection. Some common-sense parenting behaviors are challenging for me because I didn't experience them growing up, but Albert happily steps up.

"Alexa, call Sam." I hope my friend answers. The phone rings once. 'I'm sorry, the mailbox you are trying to reach is full…'

Good grief, Sam, you never let that happen. What is going on? I tap my fingers on the countertop as though it is a keyboard that will spell out an answer for me. One comes to mind.

"Alexa, call Meghan." The phone rings.

"Hello, this is Meghan. Please leave your name and number at the sound of the beep."

"Meghan, it's Blair. This is awkward, but I'm calling about Sam. Have you heard from her? It's some time since the gala, and I haven't heard a peep. You know that's not like her. She checks in every day. Well then, that's all."

Something's not right about this. Sam's had brief flings before, but that's what they were…brief! And no matter where she is, she touches base. Suddenly, my phone tweets.

"Hello?"

"Blair, it's Meghan. Sorry, I was in the bathroom. What's this about Sam disappearing?"

"I didn't say she disappeared. I said that I hadn't heard from her in a while."

"That's not, Sam. She can't help but keep in touch and share the latest news. Something is wrong."

"Well, great, just great. I wanted to know if you heard from Samantha; that's all. I don't need you to worry me even more."

"You should be worried. Did you see Sam at the Gala?"

"At the Gala? Yes. Why?"

"Have you ever seen her wear heels or platforms? She looked like a movie star hanging on the arm of a tall blond."

"Well, you know her flings. What does this have to

192

do with anything?"

"The blonde might have been Charles, and Sam told Debbie she was going off with him somewhere."

"What? Let me get this straight. You think Little Sis, who has since turned into Charles, morphed into a female again and showed up at the gala?"

"Yes. Well, Charles wore a mask. But the height, the size…"

"That's absurd… no, crazy."

"Hear me out, please."

"Why… so you can tell the police and get them all stirred up against Charles and Sam again?

"No. No, I haven't, and I won't call the law. Many influential people admire Charles. I'm trying to understand their perspective. I'm through trying to prove him guilty. It will only hurt my career like it hurt my friends.

"I'm forthright with you because, despite our recent differences, we have many years together. I love you, Sam and Debbie. I didn't mean to hurt any of you."

"Yes, well, guess what, you did, Megs. You did."

"I know that now. I'm truly sorry, but…well…"

"Spit it out."

"Girl's Night Out tried to solve the death of a puppy. We went after the perpetrator, remember?"

"Yes, that weird, perverted kid."

"Yes. We went after him until we didn't have to anymore."

"What in the world do you mean?"

"Blair, he died."

"Yes, he died. He killed himself, remember?"

"I don't think he killed himself."

"Say what?"

"Charles did it as Char back then. Remember she left us at the club early that night? I remember because it was the same night I met Will."

"Oh, for Christ's sake. I've about heard enough."

"Don't hang up. Sam is with Charles; I know it. Sam is close to Charles and knows how he got away. And now we haven't heard from her; she's vanished."

My eyes well up with tears. We stopped investigating Seth's death after Charlotte disappeared, and the police never suspected anything but suicide. Spontaneously, I throw the phone across the room, smashing into a picture window.

Albert runs into the kitchen. "Hey, what's wrong? Blair?"

"Oh, Albert, I'm afraid."

"Come on, sweetie, sit down. Tell me about it."

Between sobs, I explain Meghan's phone call.

"No wonder you are upset. I need to visit that woman."

"No. No, Albert, I'm not mad at her. I'm furious at my mother—my sick, horrible mother because Charles got her genes, but even worse. I always had questions about Regena's death, but I pushed them away. I believe Meghan, I think. She could be right. Sam may be in danger, but I have no idea what to do about it. What do I do, Albert?"

Albert becomes quiet and still, as he always does before trying to solve a problem. He pulls a chair in front of me and sits.

"Baby, if you believe Meghan on any level, we have no choice but to call the police or the FBI. Someone needs to step up for Samantha, as he may have her imprisoned in some foreign country...or worse. We need to do something about it. I'll make the call if you want."

"Yes, please, Albert. I'll answer all their questions, but the initial call… I can't do it."

****

Amelia Island Police Department

"Captain, we have a missing person complaint on Samantha Yu."

"The woman the FBI busted a couple of weeks ago when they shot and killed an actor?"

"The same, Samantha, sir. She's been missing for a few days. Friends spoke to her on the night of that big gala. She said she was going on vacation with a tall blond but would be in touch."

"So, what's the problem?"

"The person reporting her missing is none other than Blair Finney, Charles Innocenti's sister."

"Hm."

"There's more, Captain."

"Go on, Sargent."

"The sister believes the tall blonde that accompanied Samantha at the gala may have been a disguised Charles Innocenti."

"So, the FBI screwed that up too." The captain barks, "Call Homeland Security and the FBI; let them fight it out. Meanwhile, get statements from those who saw Ms. Yu last."

"That would be Debbie Williams Duke. I've been calling her, but the phone goes to voicemail."

"Well, get over there. Let's make sure Debbie Duke isn't missing either."

"Yes, Captain."

"And, Sergeant, put out a missing person APB on Samantha Yu."

Chapter 28

Charles

Carson hewed out a huge tree trunk and straddled it over cement blocks for a makeshift desk. My cushioned office chair is comfortable and the only luxury item that has traveled with me in our van throughout Africa. It's great to be home.

Yesterday, I arrived at my hut in the Goualougo Triangle, near the Dzanga River in Congo, Brazzaville. After a few hours of sleep, I have paid off my creditors. Things are back to normal, and I'm ready to implement plans to eradicate human trafficking in Thailand, a pilot program for our American infiltration.

"Agnes, where is Carson? Has he prepared my travel plans to Thailand?"

"Charles, are you sure Thailand is the best target?"

"You are questioning me, Agnes?"

"No, not really, son. It is an obvious choice. Thailand is the worst when it comes to trafficking babies, but it is an obvious place to look for someone who wants to stop it."

"Don't worry, I'm sure Sam has told everyone that I'm in South America. I'll be hunted there before Thailand."

"I doubt that." Agnes appears off-kilter as she stares at nothing, muttering to herself.

"What?"

"Oh, just thinking, son."

She said something aloud she didn't mean to say. I watch her muscles tense as I stare long and hard.

"Agnes, I lived in the jungle for years and sense when something is amiss. With humans, it's just as obvious as it is in nature. Your forehead is perspiring, and your lower lip is twitching. What aren't you telling me?"

"Oh, son, I am sorry. I am sorry. I want not to tell you."

"Tell me now, damn it."

"There was a horrible accident. A plane accident. That girl, Sam. Her plane went down right after take-off. Pilot and passenger are dead."

My heart jumps and begins to palpitate irregularly. I breathe deeply to calm it as my body starts to shake from a rage that threatens to consume me. Again, I deep breathe and stand slowly, never taking my eyes off Agnes, who is more nervous than ever. I pace around her, staring, piercing through her demeanor.

She begins to whimper. "Please, Charles. I am sorry for your loss. I know that girl was special to you."

"That girl…that girl! You ugly, calculating bitch. What did you do?" I face Agnes, place my hands around her neck, and push her back against the wall. Tightening my fingers, I feel her carotid artery pounding. I smell her fear. "I said, what did you do?"

"She causes you to lose focus, Charles. I was not certain you would even return to Africa."

My fingers tighten more. Agnes's face turns beet red. "I said, what did you do?"

Agnes gasps for air. "Explosive. Little one. It went

off early, or no one would know what happened. It was a mistake. I am sorry, Charles. I am…"

I release my grip, letting her sink to the floor, gulping in air.

"First, an innocent actor dies—not your fault, you claim. You placed Sam in danger that night, too. Did you expect gunfire would have killed her too, but you failed?" I'm not waiting for an answer.

"Do you know what you have done? All these years with me, but now your stupidity has ruined everything …you may have destroyed The Defenders and my life. You wretched piece of insanity."

"Please, Charles. Please." Agnes grovels at my feet.

"But I'm nothing but compassionate, especially after all the years of loyal service to me. Stop begging."

"Then, forgive me, I beg you, son?"

"Come, Agnes. You may hug me."

"Oh, thank you, thank you, Charles. Thank you for forgiving me. We have been together for so long. I knew my son would forgive me." She squeezes against my chest. I give her this moment of closeness I believe she's wanted for many years.

"Forgive you?" I place my hands on both sides of her head and lift her eyes to mine. "We spent fifteen years together, Agnes. You've been like a mother and have become crazy, like my mother.

"I didn't warrant protection from Regena. You see, she was confused, too. She threatened my life on multiple occasions with that damn gun pointed at my head. But do you know what happened the last time she held a gun to me, Agnes?

"I sweet-talked her. I calmed her down. I hugged her like I'm hugging you. Then I maneuvered behind her like this. I lifted her arm so the gun pointed at her head and helped her pull the trigger. I helped her to escape the hell she created; now, I'll help you."

I hear myself growl as I twist Agnes's neck with the swiftness of a wild beast. Instinctively, I bite into her throat until I draw blood. The taste of it snaps me out of my rage. After loading the body into the Land Rover, I drive over rough terrain to a baobab tree large enough to park most of the vehicle inside its trunk area. The sun shines low in the western sky—too close to nightfall. But I have no choice.

Throwing Agnes over my shoulder, I trek deeper into the wild. A lion roars, so I march, circumventing its call, respecting his right to territory. Within minutes, I stumble upon a copulating lion and lioness. "No worries, my friends. Just keep on." I understand that procreation interests them only; they will ignore me.

Soon, I hear a jackal too close for comfort. I ready a Mambele knife in my free hand. Blades protrude out of each side of the weapon, which can cause damage to multiple targets. I listen closely. The jackal sounds alone, probably a mother hunting to feed her cubs. Jackals, the pests of Africa, kill most of their food but also steal dead prey from any creature. This jackal will not have Agnes yet. I'm prepared to kill it, but only as a last resort.

I recognize the tracks of a bull elephant heading for water. I befriended him many years ago. Mixed in with elephant tracks are others—predators. But the elephant herd would protect me as one of their own.

When I reach the mana brought by the Kwilu, an outlying tributary of the Congo River, I smell the air— elephant dung. The bull hurries toward me but stops short when I speak.

"Hello, my friend. I've brought you a snack." I reach into my pocket and pull out a pile of peanuts that I pour onto the ground —the huge bull trumpets.

"Complaining? Okay, next time, I'll bring more, Samson."

I shift Agnes's weight. I'll be glad to stop carrying the corpse. But first, I examine the reeds and fronds around the pool. The mana dwindles during the dry season. No air bubbles appear in the middle of the pond —no crocodiles there or in the fronds near me. Quickly, I drop Agnes on the shore. After I slit open her belly, the smell of meat and blood attracts the hidden reptiles toward the carcass.

I back off, knowing that if the Crocs don't decimate the body, the hyenas will. I feel contempt, a loathing far beyond what I had ever experienced. I should have left Agnes alive to feel the pain of being ripped to shreds.

I killed her for you, Sam.

The first crocodile is enormous and grabs her head, dragging her entire body into the pond. I scrutinize the scene, making sure nothing of Agnes reaches the shore. Disturbed by the thrashing crocodiles, a hippo surprises me when she lifts her head out of the water. Before the hippo senses my presence, I back up slowly.

The last sound I hear is the snap of Agnes's bones breaking before bits fall to the bottom of a watery grave. I turn away and pick up my pace, surprised that I failed to notice the hippo. It could have meant my death.

Carefully, I head back toward the Land Rover as evening darkens. A thirsty leopard meets me on the trail. I remove my shirt and wave it while hollering. The leopard scurries into the cover of high grass toward the trees, more frightened of me than I am of it.

"Sam, I'm sorry for what she did to you. I wish you could see the sunset here." I stop to watch a rare neon fungus called Chimpanzee fire. It illuminates the jungle floor. The light comforted me when I first began my quest. Even from a distance, the glow still soothes me.

"Oh, Sam, you would have loved to see this."

Sunset brings predators. I feel for the boat horn inside my pocket. The loud noise scares off most maneaters, but I use it sparingly. Even though it frightens marauding wildlife, it also alerts others to my whereabouts.

A rustle to the left catches my ear. It is moving, circling behind me. I count three lionesses and hope no male travels with them. I blow the horn and wave my shirt.

"Get out of here, now. Go."

At first, they scurry off, but soon, they circle back toward me. No tree is close enough. No whistling thorns are near either. I stand exposed in waist-high grass, so I sound the horn again. The matriarch, a brave lioness who must have cubs to feed, ignores it. If a male follows her, he will help the lioness finish me off. I have no chance if I stand and fight.

"Samson. Samson." I holler, hoping the elephant arrives in time.

The lioness shows her head, pawing the ground, making ready to spring. I'm confident my Mambele will slice through her. But can I handle the two others who have become bold and back her?

My heart pounds —adrenaline courses through my body. The lioness springs toward me when Samson's trumpet sounds. The ground shakes. Somehow, I sidestep the lioness who, hearing the elephant, tries to turn mid-air. A claw swipes my arm and knocks me to the ground, where I become easy prey. The lioness tumbles into the grass and barely escapes Samson's pounding feet as he charges the trio.

The bull returns to my side, extending his trunk to help me.

"Thank you, Samson." He caresses my body before he faces the direction of the lions. He trumpets fiercely, declaring a warning before he rushes them again. Samson scares them off and returns to me, indicating he wants a scratching behind his ear, his favorite spot.

I search the pockets of my cargo shorts to feed him the remaining peanuts as I itch him. "Keep them busy, Samson."

As I near my vehicle, my flashlight illuminates two Cheetahs yawning as they lie on the four-wheeler's roof. The twin brothers jump down and sprint toward me.

"Einstein, Hawking, how are you? It's been a long time."

I appreciate their visit through clenched teeth, trying to ignore the searing pain in my arm. Each cat stands on their hind legs, hugging me, licking my ears, and sounding the chirrups that express their excitement. I had rescued the pair after a poacher killed their mother for her skin.

"You're eating well, my boys. I'm sorry, but I'm on a schedule today—no time for play. Go on, now. Go on, but stay away from Samson. He's on duty for me and in a mood."

The cheetahs protest but take off after a rustle in the bush. Strange how cheetahs take to me; even wild cheetahs don't run away. They sit and watch as I speak to them in Cheetah talk—small chirrups and purrs.

Eventually, they allow me to interact with them.

Cheetahs climb trees to see over the plains. Often, I sit with them in the same tree. Carson dubbed me a Cheetah whisperer and originated the Duma nickname, which means Cheetah in Swahili.

I wrap my injured arm tightly before turning the ignition key. "Sam, I'm sorry. You didn't deserve death." I drive to the hut, knowing that my anger caused carelessness with the hippo and lions. I had almost joined Sam this evening.

Carson's jungle hat sits on the desk inside the hut. The cherry aroma of his pipe greets me. He only smokes when working on figures. I call out to the man who has risen to a command level. He hurries to me.

"Sir?"

"Carson, you were in Mexico?"

"Yes. Of course, Duma, I picked up the rental as you instructed."

"As I instructed?"

"Yes, Duma. I ditched it in the river."

"Didn't you find that instruction odd, Carson?"

"Si, but Agnes assured me that was what you wanted before you took off for Rio."

"Brazil?"

Carson looks stymied. "Duma, Agnes informed me you were pursuing a human trafficking group there. You worried me. I wanted to be by your side for such a dangerous operation. But Agnes said you hired a crew since an assassin still watched for me there. She said you needed an explosive to blow a limo apart. So, I was glad to play some part in your endeavor. I'm glad to hear it was a success."

"Agnes told you it was a success?"

Carson stares into my eyes. "Si. Wasn't it, sir?"

"No. I knew nothing about it."

"Duma?"

"Agnes used the device for selfish motives. She killed two innocents and, in doing so, has jeopardized my entire program."

"She used my bomb…Oh, God, forgive me. Sir…who?"

"Someone I've known for many years. The very person who interested me in animal welfare, Samantha Yu, along with her, was a harmless pilot."

"Samantha called Sam—yes, I've heard Agnes complain about her. She said Sam might prevent you from returning to us. I told her it was nonsense, that your vision rose above everyone and everything. I thought that was the end of it; I brushed it off, Duma, so I'm to blame. I made the bomb, although I thought it odd. I'm…"

"Carson, I do not blame you. I trusted Agnes even though her plans caused another innocent's death before Sam. I gave my employee the benefit of the doubt; I shouldn't have. My trust, my mistake killed Sam."

Carson pounds the table with his hands. "I want…I need to confront her and tell Agnes I hate her for this! The Defenders do not kill innocent people. Agnes needs elimination."

"No worries, Carson. The Crocs deal with her as we speak."

"Duma, I wish you had ordered me to do it."

"This was personal. Besides, a more important role awaits you. I'm appointing you as The Defender's new leader. You understand the training system on all levels, including the fiscal trail. I am confident in your skills."

"But what of you? You just returned from the States. Why are you leaving?"

"If I don't, Defenders could die under Agnes's cursed actions. Everyone will believe I killed Sam if they don't already. I must surrender to authorities to prove otherwise. The Defenders must survive."

"Si, you are correct, of course, if there is no other way."

I think quickly. "I will notify everyone by the emergency alert email system."

"Yes, of course, Duma."

To: The Defenders
From: Duma

Actions taken by a high-level defender, without my authority and my knowledge, could destroy all the work we have accomplished in fifteen-plus years. The person whom you have known as Agnes has killed three innocent people for personal, selfish reasons. An unacceptable act like hers reaps what it sows; do not expect to hear from her again, as we, The Defenders, never use our skills to kill innocents.

"To save The Defender's reputation, I must answer for her atrocities. Too many mothers have died to promote our organization; I will not allow them to die in vain because of a jealous woman's actions. Stand fast, no matter what you hear about me. As you know, our system protects not only the animals and Africa's children, but it protects you and your families, too. Remember, if one Defender falls, the organization protects their families. Don't let anyone tear our system apart.

"I appoint Carson as your new acting leader. Have

complete faith in him as I do. He will implement our human trafficking quest. Remember to treat traffickers the same as you do poachers, without mercy. I'm counting on you. I am humbled to have led you all these years. I wish success for The Defenders, as there is no other choice.

Remember to pass this notice along to volunteers without internet access.

Work hard, and good luck,

Duma.

I push send. There is no turning back. Carson dresses my arm without asking. He pours alcohol on the wound and utilizes butterfly bandages to close the gap, then wraps it.

"You had a run-in with a lion, Duma. But it could have been worse, sir."

"It's nothing. Carson, do one last thing for me."

"Si, of course." Carson stands at attention, his crimson face flushed from his anger and rage toward Agnes. Like a balloon, he may burst, but in front of me.

"Rent a plane to take me to Johannesburg. I'll visit the safe house there. Then, I'll fly first class to Miami, with an immediate connection to Jacksonville."

"Yes, sir. Under what name?"

"Good question. Let's utilize Leslie Heinz, our favorite rich gal."

"Excellent, sir." I open my laptop to iMessages.

Dearest Meghan:

I heard the news about Sam's death today. I can assure you that the individual responsible for her death has been dealt with severely and is no longer a member of The Defenders.

Even though I am not connected to Sam's death, I must take responsibility so people do not lose trust in my organization. That is why I am returning to the United States. I must broadcast the truth, letting the people hear from me directly.

I will require a proficient defense attorney; I want only you, Meghan.

Tell me I can count on your cooperation.

With regret,

Charles

Ten minutes later, I receive a reply.

Yes. For Blair, I will defend you.

Hm. Short and sweet. Megs has the right idea.

"Carson, there is a file marked history in the safe house in case anything happens to me. I want my sister to understand how I accomplished what I have—how I adapted to the jungle and implemented my program. You'll see to it one day?"

Carson hands me an itinerary and passports with shaky hands. "Si, of course, Duma …"

I cut him off. "From this moment on, Carson, The Defenders is your responsibility. I'm on my own now. Goodbye."

I don't bother with formalities. I do not shake hands. Even after Carson's loyal years of service, I can walk out the door and never look back.

Then, why, oh why, does Sam invade my brain like a virus?

Chapter 29

My private locker in Johannesburg stores all my essential disguises. Jumping back and forth from male to female keeps authorities guessing. My trip to the States must not be jeopardized, so I dress carefully. Leslie requires natural pearl earrings with a matching necklace, an auburn wig, and a flowing blouse with tight jeans underneath—a tailored yet feminine look. A pair of flat designer boots will complete the ensemble.

My carry-on holds toiletries and a change of clothes for Jacksonville. Flying to the States without at least one piece of booked luggage would cause suspicion, so I fill the second bag with resort wear...male.

I must speak to Meghan before I surrender to the law or before they find me. This might be my last deception - ever. As I settle into the first-class seat, Sam's smile flashes before me. I recite my mantra: *Don't think about it.* I deep breathe to calm my body and mind and turn down offers of alcohol from the stewardess, sipping on a bottle of Perrier instead.

I stretch out in my seat, waiting patiently for passengers to board. The jungle requires both patience and speed. Although I'm relaxed, sleep eludes me. I ruminate about Sam, our trip to Africa together, the touch of her lips, and the sincere love I had seen in her eyes. I can't turn off the visual of her, and it fills me with anger. I make use of the rage, funneling it into hatred toward the women I wish to kill repeatedly: Agnes, responsible for Sam's death, and Regena, accountable for creating me.

Half the passengers disembark in Miami. A few remain seated as the plane continues to Jacksonville and on to their destination, New York City.

Suddenly, emptiness possesses me. I'm a blank—nothing to do, nothing to manage, useless. I curse the woman who ruined the life I created. I shoot off a text.

—Hi Meghan—

—How about this afternoon for an early dinner? I'll pick you up, okay? If Blair can make it, I'd like that too.—

A return text states:

—We'll be waiting, Leslie.—

I switch to another program designed to scan Meghan's home and outside grounds. Hidden cameras from the last visit when Sam lived are still transmitting. I also had a crew bug Meghan's phone. I adjust my earplugs and turn up the volume.

"Blair, it's Meghan."

"What now?" My sister sounds short-tempered.

"We have an early dinner tonight with an old friend."

"An old friend? Oh. Is it booked in a public forum, a busy restaurant?"

"I'll make certain it will be. Meanwhile, William stayed home today. So, let our friend pick us up at my house. Come on by about four."

Early dinner? Public forum?

"I'll be there earlier. I may break my alcohol fast for this one. Have some wine ready, Megs."

"Still a Pinot Noir gal?"

"As long as it's decent, I'll drink it. My nerves are a wreck over this, you know. I'm a real Mexican jumping bean."

"I'll surprise you with a bottle I've been saving for a special occasion."

"By the way, is Debbie coming?"

"He didn't ask for Debbie. Just the two of us. Why?"

"I won't drink in front of her out of respect."

"I understand. That's wise and kind. See you soon."

Blair hangs up without saying goodbye.

Our meeting could go badly. Blair and Meghan don't trust me—wanting to talk in public. I type in more commands and pull up Debbie's estate. I zero into the house by the front door, where an emergency vehicle parks, engine running.

"Please hurry. My wife is dying." Greg shows the EMTs up the stairs to the bedroom; I slide the screen over to follow them.

He asks them, "Do any of you have A-negative blood? The hospital is always running short."

A-negative? That's why she has been waiting? I focus close to Debbie's face. It glows with a deep yellow hue. "Jaundice," I whisper. Debbie's breathing is quick and shallow. She has more money than one could ever dream of, yet she cannot save herself with it. She out-drank all the ladies during GNO. She maintained her drinking back then, but it must have escalated over the years.

Debbie's health requires a savior, but will there be enough time?

****

Greg - Three Years Earlier

"Greg, my stomach hurts… it hurts something

210

awful."

"Sweetheart, you feel cold, but you're sweating." I keep my hand on her forehead. "How can you be sweating when you are cold as ice?"

"Call nine-one-one." Suddenly, my Debbie faints, but I catch her before she hits the floor. After I lay her on the couch, I punch nine-one-one.

"Debbie, sweetie, hold on. Help is on the way." The ambulance arrives in minutes, but it seems like hours as I dab my wife's face with a cool cloth. As she comes to, the ER doctor asks questions while palpating her midriff.

"Ow. Please don't do that again," she moans.

I can't stand to see the love of my life in pain.

A nurse draws tubes of blood and carries them to the lab. It helps to be a significant contributor to the hospital when one becomes sick. Meanwhile, my wife gets a liver scan. Her diagnosis comes quickly.

"Your wife has hepatitis C, Mr. Duke. Worse than that, her liver is severely damaged; there is no coming back from it."

"What? What does that mean?"

"It means that without a liver transplant, your wife will die." Doctor Berkholder talks to me while looking over his horn-rimmed spectacles. "We're admitting her. We'll work on strengthening your wife and help her through the inevitable alcohol withdrawal."

"Dear God."

"To receive a transplant, your wife must stop drinking for six months. We'll keep her comfortable with regular blood transfusions during the interim, but that's the other problem."

"You mean it gets worse?"

"It's difficult, as she has A-negative blood. It isn't

the rarest blood type, but only six percent of the population has it. We keep a supply here right now, but to maintain stock, I recommend you search for more blood donors locally as the hospital does."

The doctor keeps his voice level but firm. "Do you have any questions?"

"Yes. How does Debbie's rare blood affect the chances of receiving a liver?"

"*If* your wife stops drinking for six months, and I mean not even a sip of alcohol, *if* someone dies after those six months, and *if* that someone is an A-negative donor, it will go to rank number one on the list. When she is at the top of the list, she will receive the liver—again, if no alcohol is in her system."

I shake my head. "There are too many ifs, Doctor."

"The good news is, since the donor has a rare blood type, and few require A-negative, Mrs. Duke has a decent chance. Right now, she is receiving a blood transfusion. We'll treat Hep C as best we can. If everything goes well, it should help sustain life until a liver becomes available."

"Another if. Doc, Debbie is my life. I can't lose her. Do all you can, please."

"I understand. Your wife is my priority. We don't forget our benefactors, Mr. Duke. I will do everything in my power to help her stabilize."

"Thank you. Okay, to see her now?"

"Hospital policy usually prohibits families from being in the transfusion rooms, but your wife is a special patient. Yes, seeing you would be a big help. Come on; I'll accompany you back there."

"I appreciate it."

I wipe away a tear before the doctor sees it, trying to

lighten my mood for Debbie's sake—the woman I won fifteen years before. She needs me desperately now. I smile when I see her, trying to ignore the blood pumping into her arm.

"Hey, good-looking. I'm here." Debbie opens her oversized baby blues with heavy eyelids.

"Greg. I blew it, didn't I?" Her voice is weak, with a wavy sound like a creaky door in a horror film.

"What are you talking about, babe? You didn't screw up anything. Health setbacks sometimes happen. This transfusion will bring you around. Don't worry. The doctors will fix this."

"Liar." She tries to smile.

"I'm not lying, babe. We're a team, remember? You hurt and feel like crap, but it's only up from here, I promise you."

I caress her hair, trying to instill stamina and backbone through every pore in her head. "I'm with you every step of the way."

True to my word, I terminate work on a novel and cancel all editing jobs. I spend an exorbitant amount of time with her, cognizant that she sometimes covets solitude. Obsession overcomes me. My wife is stuck with me.

"Greg, if ever there is a face I want to see before my last breath, it is yours. But, honey, you need your rest, too."

Before the hospital releases her, I pull the doctor aside on the sly. "Doc, you know how wealthy Debbie is. Surely, a healthy donation could move her up the transplant list."

He puts his arm around me. "Although the hospital would happily accept a donation for the new wing, I'm sorry. No, it won't increase one's standing on the waitlist. I don't blame you for trying. I would, too, if my wife were ill. But the system doesn't work that way, not even for a surgeon's wife.

"And, if you think about going to another hospital with the same offer, I must warn you that their answer will be the same. No reputable hospital would change the list based on money. If you go anywhere but a renowned hospital, the liver and the entire operation would be questionable. You want Debbie to have the best of the best, correct?"

"Of course I do. I'm desperate, Doc."

"I understand. All I can say is have faith. And keep the alcohol away from her. Anytime tests find it in her system, she loses placement on the list and must earn the right to get back on...at the bottom. She doesn't have time for that."

"I'll be a Nazi about that. She won't consume a drop of alcohol."

"Fair enough. Time is short for all of us. It's much shorter for your wife. She needs that new liver as soon as possible."

"Yes, I understand your position."

Already, I'm preparing to battle for the love of my life.

Chapter 30

Charles - Present-Day

Remotely, I watch the rescue crew lift Debbie onto the stretcher and carry her to the ambulance. I'm indebted to her. And I can help. *Debbie, hold on.*

A rental awaits me at JAX airport—not exactly nondescript, Carson. The red Mustang is speedy and comfortable. Following the GPS, I speed to Meghan's house, where she answers the door.

"Hello, Leslie, is it?"

"Meghan, no time for hellos. Blair, let's go. We're off to the hospital. Debbie is near death."

I throw my wig to the couch and strip off my blouse. A man's tee shirt is underneath. I pull out the breast pads and jump into a pair of less-fitted jeans.

"You aren't going anywhere, Mr. Innocenti." An FBI agent steps out of the hallway with a badge in hand. "We have questions to ask you."

I pull a makeup remover from my pocket. "I'll answer all your questions, but not now. I match Debbie's rare blood type. I'm giving her half my liver. We have no time to spare."

"He's not lying." Blair stares at me, astounded at my offer. "She needs a liver transplant. You are A-negative, Charles?"

"Yes. We are wasting time."

"That's true." Meghan's turn to convince the agent. "He won't disappear on a gurney with half a liver, will he? Besides, I told you that he came over to hand himself in. As his attorney, I'll stand for him. Why don't you give all of us a ride to the hospital and validate the facts there? You can help us save a life."

"I can do that. Let's go." We are an anxious group piling into the agent's sedan. He places a flashing light on top and takes off.

Blair speed-dials Greg. "We have a match. Do you hear me? We have a match from a live donor. It's Charles Innocenti, my brother. He's A-Rh negative. I don't know why I didn't know that before, but we're on the way. Yes, now. Half a liver is better than no liver.

"Tell the doctors to prepare Debbie for surgery. Tell them Charles is the originator of The Defenders, so they take us seriously. Be there in minutes!"

The ten-minute drive seems like an eternity as emotions run like roller-coasters inside the agent's car.

"If this is an attempt to win our sympathy, Mr. Innocenti, you will be mistaken."

"Just deliver me to the hospital, agent." I'm irritated that Blair has "outed" me to hospital personnel. The agent begins to speak, but Blair cuts him off.

"Not now! Not now! For heaven's sake, our best friend is near death. I don't want to hear the arguing. I don't want to hear anything." Meghan pulls Blair close as she sobs. The agent steps on the gas, and we arrive at the hospital within minutes. A crew awaits us outside with a wheelchair.

"Mr. Innocenti, please sit. Before proceeding, we must match your type and ensure you are healthy. There are a lot of papers to sign."

"Check the blood, people, and get me into that room. I verbally appoint Meghan as my power of attorney. She may sign all the papers for me as I agree one hundred percent to donating half my liver. You all heard that. You are all witnesses, and that includes an FBI agent. It should cut your prep time down. We have a life to save.

"Meghan, no photos of me are permitted."

The orderlies speed me down the hallway as I lift my hands to cover my face. Whispers increase. "The Defenders … he started The Defenders …donating…hero… God bless him."

****

Blair

As orderlies lift Debbie to another gurney, Doctor Berkholder quickly updates Greg and me.

"We've given her two transfusions. She's come around well enough to operate. But it will be dangerous as she isn't as strong as I'd like her to be."

"We both know she'll die if you don't proceed, Doc. Debbie's more indestructible than you think. Go ahead. Do it."

Greg speaks courageously, but I'm afraid I may lose my brother, my best friend …or both.

The doctor nods. "The donated liver is ready, and it is incredibly healthy."

Before staff wheels Debbie into surgery, Greg whispers in her ear. "Babe, it's Greg. I'm here. Blair is, too. We have a perfect match for you. So, you hang on, okay? Soon, you'll be as good as new. Promise me, sweetheart, that you will hang on."

A small tear trickles down my friend's cheek.

"That better be a happy tear, babe. I'll see you soon. I love you, babe. See you soon."

The orderlies wheel Debbie into the unknown, and Greg leans against the wall, weak from worry. I had insisted on escorting him to Debbie's side, rules be damned. Suddenly, I remember Charles. Had anyone held his hand or whispered sweet words in his ear before surgery?

I shrug, understanding that he thrives on being alone. Autonomy carries him nearer to nature's pulse, the throb of the universe, or so Charlotte mentioned years ago. Still, guilt grips me for not having escorted him or thanked him. I'll take care of my apologies later. I can only focus on my best friend and kindred spirit as if my thoughts had the power to heal.

****

Twelve hours later, Doctor Berkholder steps into the waiting room and smiles. "Mr. Duke, Debbie came through like a champion. She's fine, but the first two weeks will tell if the body accepts or rejects the liver."

Greg sighs loudly and turns to give us a thumbs up. "She's fine; she's fine."

Albert, Meghan, Will, and I cheer. Without warning, Gregory breaks down and cries. Ever the gentleman, Albert hurries over and man-hugs him. "Tense situation, Greg."

"I don't know what I would have done if I lost her. She is my life."

"Well, you haven't lost her, my friend. She's a fighter; you know that."

Greg nods. "Yes, yes, that's true. And now for step two. Let's pray her body accepts the liver."

"We will pray. We can all offer our private prayers. There's a chapel here somewhere."

Greg shakes his head. "You go on, Meghan. I'm

going to the ICU to see Deb and tell her the good news when she opens her eyes."

The exhausted surgeon patiently watches our interactions, but then he raises an eyebrow. "By the way, the donor is fine, too. He donated a strong, healthy liver. We should all be grateful."

"Yes, of course." I blush. "We were so worried about Debbie... I didn't think. When will he wake up?"

"He's been awake for some time. I'll send a staff member to escort you to his room. Meanwhile, Greg, follow me. Debbie's overall condition has improved already with a strong heartbeat and..." A security door closes behind Greg as our group lets out a collective sigh.

"I don't know about you, but Will and I want time in the chapel. We will pray that Debbie's body accepts this gift. Want to join us?"

"Meghan, if I step into a chapel, I'll burst into flames. Besides, I should be here for Charles. How about you, Albert?" I urge my spiritual husband to join them. "I'd like to see my brother alone for now."

"You've got it, sweetheart. If you need me, text, for heaven's sake...no pun intended." Albert leans in and kisses me sweetly before trailing Meghan and Will.

I park in the waiting room, wondering, arguing, and muttering aloud. Charles wouldn't have returned if he was guilty of murder. He couldn't have killed that boy. Or maybe this is a smart way to outmaneuver the law. I know how he felt about Sam, but ...

"Mrs. Finney, we transferred Charles to his room if you want to see him."

The nurse startles me. "Yes," I say half-heartedly, unsure whether I should believe anything Charles says.

"We nurses are proud to have your brother here. I

give monthly to The Defenders fund. What a productive organization, and to think we have the elusive creator at our hospital. Well, I'm tickled over it. Your brother changed the world. No poacher assumes he can slaughter anymore, not without losing their own lives in the process.

"Finally, offshoots of the original Defenders have surfaced here in the states to protect the wolves, wild horses, buffaloes, bears, wild cats."

"No, they haven't, according to Charles. They aren't a part of his group."

"Well, whatever; no hunter dares to point a rifle into a hibernating bear's cave and open fire, killing mamas and cubs—consequences are too dire. No-kill animal shelters are springing up everywhere, too. I wish I had the guts to be on the front lines. But I'm a nurturer more than a…a…"

"Killer? Murderer?"

Her insulted eyes pierce me. "I don't label anyone with negative names whose agenda and motivation protects our God-given wildlife. They are champions who deter atrocities—superheroes who defy pathetic systems that acknowledge the slaughter of innocent creatures yet do nothing. The planet restores to its natural balance thanks to The Defenders."

"You believe that, don't you?"

"Don't you? He's your blood, for goodness sake!"

"I can't deny that Charles's process has saved many species."

"Oh, he's accomplished more than that. Humanity's loving nature surfaces unafraid, thanks to him. Soon, a world of kindness will rule. Everyone believes that. Some of us regard Charles as a prophet. Well, here is his room."

Whew. Enough of her drama. I plaster on a smile.

"Charles, you have company," the nurse says too sweetly.

"Blair. You came." Charles is groggy.

"Of course, I'm here. How are you feeling?" *A prophet? A fucking prophet?*

"Puny and achy. I told the doctor to forget the pain pills."

"Charles, there's no need for heroism after surgery. There is nothing to prove now. Take the pain meds."

"No, Blair. I use a lot of energy. Meds will slow me down. I insist nothing incapacitates my thought processes." He mumbles in a whisper.

"No, nothing but giving away half your liver." I pat his hand, grateful that he has saved my best friend in the world.

"Yes, for Debbie. I doubt if I would do it for anyone else except for Sam and you, of course. I respect Debbie, and I owe her. She raised enough funds to start the human trafficking program in various countries. It was the least I could do. I'd have done it sooner if I had known we were the same blood type."

"You didn't inherit it from Mom. So, you must have your father's. Hmm. How did you learn that she needed A negative?"

"Surveillance. I spied on Debbie at the right moment. Greg mentioned A-negative to the EMTs."

"This is one time I'm glad you snooped and cared to help. Could you have helped Sam?" I couldn't resist the question. It burned a hole in my brain.

"Sam. My poor Sam. I'd kill myself before harming her. She loved me, you know. Sending her back to the

States was for her reputation and her well-being. Law agencies here would show no mercy to anyone connected with me. Blair, I swear on everything holy that I did not cause that explosion.

"But a sick member of my entourage did. She was jealous, eliminating Sam like garbage, like a poacher. She didn't deserve that."

"No, *our* Sam didn't deserve death. So, what happened to the murderer?"

"Don't ask about her. I can assure you that she won't be a threat to anyone else I care about, like you, Meghan, and Debbie."

"How about the boy, Charles?"

"Ice chips. Do you mind?" I pour a few chips into his hand. He crunches a palmful. "Boy?"

"Yes, the crazy teen killer. After you disappeared, they finally found the forensics to base the fire on his actions. Everyone thought it was a stretch at the time."

"No, Meghan believed it was a stretch, but the rest of us thought he did it. I'm glad the law proved it was him." He lays his head back down on the pillow and yawns.

"Oh, no, you don't. Don't pretend you are too tired to give me answers."

"I gave half my liver away. I'm going to feel tired for some time."

"I want an answer. Did you kill Seth Overmeyer?"

"No. I did not kill him. There you have it. I'm not the cold-hearted killer you think I am. Do you feel safe with me now?"

I exhale, relieved. "Thank you. Thank you for answering that question; I believe you. I had to know for sure."

"Me too. I hoped for certainty, too." The same FBI agent who drove us to the hospital stands inside the door, holding a small recorder. "What about the person that you claimed had exploded that plane? What do you mean everyone is safe from her now?"

"You may ask. That doesn't mean I'm going to answer."

"I suggest you do, sir. Or you will be arrested on suspicion of murder."

"Agent, first, I would be arrested and tried in Mexico or Africa, not here. Florida is not in your jurisdiction for that disaster. Now, if you don't mind, I'm weak and in quite a bit of pain." My brother depresses the buzzer. "Nurse, more ice, please."

A voice comes through the speaker in seconds. "Yes, sir. Right away." A nurse scurries in, delighted to serve him like he is some rock star.

"No one else gets service like that in this hospital. What gives?" The agent scratches his head.

Now, I'm irked. "Agent, my brother finished answering your questions. If you don't realize it, Charles is a hero to many people. He saved species from mutilation, abuse, and extinction. Maybe you don't appreciate his efforts, but I do.

"Besides, he just donated half his liver to save a life, a very distinguished life. I insist you let us alone."

The agent turns off the recorder. "I admire him, m'am. I'm just following orders. Still, before he slips out, he says, "Tomorrow, Mr. Innocenti. I'll be back."

Chapter 31

I'm afraid I'm not good company for my brother after the FBI finished drilling him, adding a promise to return the next day.

The pretty nurse trots into the room again to pack the incision with ice. "I wish you could look out the window, Charles. Paparazzi, news crews, and fans in general are here wishing you well."

"Hm. Nurse, be a dear, allow a few film crews in, would you?"

"What? Are you serious?"

"I wanted a break from that annoying agent. But a film crew? I can muster up the strength."

The nurse jumps in, excited to play a part in helping The Defenders, I suppose.

"I can let them in through the garage, sir; sneak them up to your room before anyone knows they're here."

"Perfect, nurse... what is your name?"

"Aurora."

"A beautiful name, too. Please do that, Aurora. Allow a few major stations, enough to fill up the room."

The nurse practically flies out of the room.

"What the heck are you up to?"

"Instead of telling my truth one person at a time, I'll tell the world in one announcement. Then I'll be done with it. You do realize that my murderous employee jeopardized The Defenders and my legacy when she killed Sam and Jose, the pilot. I must explain."

"Yes, I suppose you do. But right now?"

"Unless you want to be on TV with me, you better vacate the room."

I stand to leave but think better of it. "No. A family sticks together. Albert taught me that. I'll find a spot in the corner and sink into it."

"Thanks…sis."

Charles tries to sit up and winces in pain.

"Don't sit. I'll adjust the bed so you aren't quite flat on your back."

"Blair, give me your scarf. The world mustn't see my whole face. Incognito serves a purpose."

I tie my scarf gingerly around his head and face like a burqa. When I finish, only his eyes show. Within minutes, news crews file into the room, each vying for an ideal spot to film. Having been warned by the nurse, they remain unusually quiet.

Once situated, Charles raises his hand. "My voice is weak from surgery so you may have to adjust your sound. I'm going to make a statement. I will not be answering questions.

"My name is Charles Innocenti. Yes, I originated The Defenders. Everything you've heard about my organization is probably correct. We eliminate poachers. However, something is about to surface that may have people questioning my organization, motives, and followers.

"Weeks ago, my dearest friend, Samantha Yu, and her pilot, Jose Ramirez, died in a plane crash. Those two people were supporters, not poachers or human traffickers. They were innocents. When I pressed an employee as to what happened, she admitted to planting an explosive on their plane out of sheer jealousy for my friendship with Samantha."

Charles gives the film crews time to digest the news. Gasps and disbelief show on their faces. Once they settle down, he continues.

"Again, my employee, Agnes, did this for no other reason than envy. As I said, I do not order the elimination of innocents, let alone someone who loved me very much and whom I held in high esteem. It is not The Defender's way.

"Still, I must take responsibility for my employee's actions. That is what I want the world to know. I implore everyone not to blame The Defenders for the heinous act of one employee. This completes my statement."

"What happened to the lady who planted the bomb?" An ambitious journalist asks.

I spring out of my chair. "My brother is not answering any more questions. You should know that only hours ago, he donated half his liver to a dear friend of mine. He saved Debbie Williams-Duke's life. Please let him rest."

"But we'd like to know…" A sudden barrage of questions comes at me until a voice booms.

"Vacate the room now, or I'll have security on you." Dr. Berkholder stands in the doorway, pointing the way down the hall. "I don't want to see any of you in this hospital again."

As the crew shuffles out, the doctor towers over my brother. "Charles, I suggest you sleep instead of holding press conferences. The possibility of infection is a reality for both donor and receiver. I'm allowing family only to see you. Do you understand, nurse? No matter what, family only."

"Yes, Doctor, I apologize. I understand perfectly."

"How long before you discharge me?" I untie the scarf from his head.

"Good grief, you are tough —no pain medications and ready to leave. I hate to disappoint you, but there is a protocol to follow as a donor that you 'couldn't be bothered hearing before the operation. So, here it is: You will remain with us for about a week. After four days, you will start feeling like your old self. The bowel function should begin then, too.

"Realize that for your liver to return to eighty percent of its size, you must eat correctly, do a bit of walking, and get fresh air the first six weeks. You will not do anything more taxing—no lifting more than five lbs. Your liver will return to ninety percent of its size by eight weeks. Your body needs plenty of rest during regeneration.

"After we discharge you, I'll see you here in a week for a checkup. Believe me, Charles, you won't feel wholly well until four to six months. So, no acrobatics, no heroism. Just normal living. Again, if you see any signs of infection or discharge once you leave, you are to call the hospital immediately. I will make time, day or night. For now, you will lay here, allow my nurses to spoil you, and recoup your strength."

"Very well. I'm too tired to argue, anyway."

"Sleep is what you need. Your body, your liver, requires quiet time. I'll check in come morning." The doctor checks his watch.

I thank him profusely as Charles falls asleep, mumbling, "Sam."

"Will someone notify me when he wakes up, please?" I ask the head nurse.

"Certainly. But your brother will sleep through the night thanks to his attorney's new directive."

"What directive is that?"

"Pain meds and sleep agents are allowed. His attorney feels he cannot make decisions for his own good. So, as I said, don't expect a call until morning. Don't worry; we nurses are all in love with him. We won't take our eyes off of him through the night."

As I leave, the nurse injects meds into the IV. "Goodnight, sweet prince."

Has anyone checked for a penis? They call Charles "him," but had he completed the whole anatomical transformation of a sex change? Is he now indeed a he? I chastise myself because it doesn't matter in the scheme of things. Charles is Charles.

Still, I'm curious.

Chapter 32

Greg

I rest on my wife's bed with her hand in mine. I can't stand separation from my beautiful gal. A beeping heart monitor lulls me into a semi-snooze in the private I.C.U. Suddenly, I feel movement, then a squeeze.

"Hey. Hey, babe. I'm here, and the operation was a success. You hear me? The operation went perfectly. Your cheeks are beginning to see patches of pink, and you feel nice and warm—good circulation, hon."

"Mmm." Debbie tries to talk, although she is intubated, but she quickly falls back to sleep. I'm relieved but concerned at the same time.

"Nurse, she woke up for a few moments, then fell asleep. Is that all right?"

"Perfectly normal. Your wife's body has been through a lot. I'll note it in her chart, though. Why don't you go home and get some real sleep? I'll call if there is a change."

"Sorry. You're stuck with me. I'm not leaving my wife. Period. Remember, there are no visiting hour rules here. You can't throw me out."

"Well, how about I bring you a cup of coffee and a snack?"

"That sounds perfect, Nurse. Thank you."

****

FBI

"Innocenti threw quite a news conference, Agent."

"Yes, Director. Unfortunately, I left before Charles made a statement directly to me. But I do have him saying that Samantha Yu's murderer was taken care of somehow."

"That isn't much. We can't do anything but notify the Mexican and South African authorities to see if an employee is missing. He could have fired her, that's all. Until we have more, I suggest you stay away from Charles. He's too well loved and worshiped. We can monitor his actions clandestinely. Period."

"But, sir-"

"You heard me, Agent."

"Yes, sir. I'll leave him alone."

Director picks up the phone and opens his contacts, selecting one. "Taylor. It's Director Marcus. I require your assistance. I want you to dig discreetly. Yes. Charles Innocenti, The Defenders' founder, employed Agnes in South Africa. No last name was mentioned. She betrayed him and may have killed an American woman and her pilot. Locate her or find any news of her whereabouts.

"I appreciate it, Taylor. Say hello to the Mrs. for me. Goodbye."

****

Blair - Four Days Post-Op

"Oh, my. It smells wonderful in here." Flower bouquets and stuffed animals fill Charles's hospital room. "Hi, Charles."

My brother nods. "Blair."

"What is all this about?"

"Fans. The broadcast rallied a lot of supporters for

The Defenders. I hear people want us in the States and are requesting entrance into my organization, which is remarkable considering all your gun laws. Your comment about donating half my liver helped."

"Well, you look a lot better, brother. Lots of color in your cheeks. How are you feeling?"

"Much more alert. I'm ready to leave this room. People must follow my specific protocols to be part of The Defenders. Unfortunately, Meghan stopped by to say she is still my power of attorney and will not allow me to leave until my doctor agrees to it."

"Oh, dear. I suppose you should have mentioned an expiration date for the directive."

"I was busy saving a life at the time. Well, you know what they say. No good deed goes unpunished."

"I'll speak to Meghan, who's only concerned for your well-being. Still, I'll talk to her about ending that agreement. Besides, you will stay with me until the doctor releases you from his care."

"I'm not waiting six months to work. I have the trafficking program implemented in Thailand, but it's new, a stepping-stone to begin elsewhere. I must help my employees enforce it."

"Hm. Maybe I should rethink that talk with Meghan." Charles raises an eyebrow. "Don't worry. I'm only kidding. Still, you must follow the Doctor's 'protocol' to stay healthy and lead anyone."

"True enough. Just talk to Meghan or, better yet, get her in here so I can give her a piece of my mind. I want this pain medication stopped, too! She's had her way with me. I want the meds to end."

"I'll tell her that. Ah, you know that human trafficking has become a huge moneymaker in this country, too. You can work on that during your six months with my family. Start running things here in the States while you recover at my house."

I reach into my shopping bag. "Since it is day four, I took the liberty of bringing your laptop. I cleaned it up with alcohol; it should be germ-free. That should help you pass the time." I put it on his bed.

My brother smiles like a kid at Christmas. "*That* I appreciate. Now, if you will excuse me, I have work to do."

"Work?"

"You are correct about human trafficking in the States. I can start setting a precedent here to save the kids. Go on, now. Let me get to it."

"Yeah? Be like that. I'll visit Debbie; she loves my company."

"Send my regards."

I blow my brother a kiss as I head out the door, smiling, practically skipping down the hallway to Debbie's room, where I peek before entering. One never knows what one might find between the two perpetual lovebirds.

Greg sits beside Debbie, watching a National Geographic Wildlife program on the bed.

"Blair, where have you been? You're late," Greg laughs.

"Late for what?"

"Oh, just late. Debbie's been bitching about your whereabouts."

"I was missing you. Tell me, how is Charles?"

I squeeze her hand. "Well, he is back to being Charles. I brought his computer. He's treating it like gold; mentally, I believe he's back in defender land. He wanted nothing to do with me when he got his hands on it. But he did send his regards."

"When he's ready, have him visit me so I can thank him personally. Doctors won't let me leave my space yet."

"Debbie, your facial tone is almost normal again. Your cheeks are pink. I haven't seen that in a long, long time. I do believe you are on the mend."

"Yes, thanks to Charles. I want to help him with any legal fees if he needs it. Or with anything else for that matter." Tears stream down Debbie's face.

Greg grabs a box of tissues. "Don't mind my weepy lady. The nurse says emotionalism is common after transplants."

"But it isn't like me," Debbie sobs.

"Oh, dear, I wish I had this gal on film. No one would believe it."

"Don't you dare. Come, hug me." Debbie continues to sniffle.

"My pleasure." I wrap my arms around her gingerly and kiss her head.

"Blair, how about I score some fresh coffee from the cafeteria?" Greg asks.

"Sure. Cream and sugar, please."

"I'll be right back, babe." He kisses his bride, and she begins to wail again.

"I don't deserve you."

He winks and quickly escapes the one thing he can't seem to handle: his wife's crying, especially without her having an apparent reason.

"Whatever can I do for you, my friend?"

"Absolutely nothing." Just like that, the waterworks stop. "Getting Greg to leave is almost impossible. The only way I can do it is to start crying. It is easier after the surgery."

"You little minx. Greg loves you to pieces."

"Sure, but I need to breathe, and that is one thing he can't or won't understand about me."

I sit on the edge of her bed. "Well, I guess you are coming around then."

"Damn straight, I am. I'd be happy if I could convince the doctors that I need to see more than these four walls."

"Yes, well, you better get used to it. You will be here for some time."

"What? Greg says I won't be in here long. You want to tell me the real deal?"

"Oh, dear, you won't like it. Depending on your condition, the hospital stay runs anywhere from two more weeks to eight weeks."

"Eight fucking weeks more? Good God." Debbie begins to shed real tears.

"You were close to death when you came in. Your body needs extra time to recover. So, replace the exasperation with thankfulness –you are alive… be grateful."

"Now you sound like Greg, but he wouldn't tell me the protocol—the coward. I am grateful. Thanks to your brother, Greg and I will continue past this setback to enjoy many more years together."

"There you go. I took the liberty of bringing your computer, too. I wiped it down with alcohol: it's germ-free. At least it will give you something to do while you are here."

"You are the sweetest. I'll continue to help Charles if I can stay awake long enough. Damn, medications make me sleepy."

"It's only day four. The doctor told Charles that your liver needs rest and time to regenerate. So, rest already. Tell Gregg to keep the coffee. My kids have a half-day of school today. It's time to wear the chauffeur hat."

Debbie smiles, already half asleep. "Next time, girlfriend. It's nice to be alive."

****

FBI

"Hello, Taylor. What do you have for me?"

"I'm afraid it isn't good news, Director."

"Give me what you have."

"The Defender volunteers and employees go by a first name only. No one knows if it is their real name or not. Agnes's passports must have been aliases if her name is even Agnes.

"As a personal favor to you, my men and I traveled the bush and showed various passport photos of her to numerous tribes. Only one remote clan recognized her, not by her face but by the wild mane of black hair streaked with an unusual white pattern in the center."

"Why only the hair?"

"It is attached to a skull they had pulled out of the belly of an exceptionally menacing crocodile. The tribe hung the skull in the shaman's house for good luck."

"The hair is an exact match to Agnes's passport photo?"

"An exact match, sir. I'm surprised she didn't color her hair like most women her age. Anyway, proof as to how she died isn't there. Tribesmen insist a crocodile ripped off the head from the torso, as proved by the jagged teeth marks on the remaining neck bone. I don't know if she was alive or dead when that happened. The rest of her could be digested in other crocs or any predatory beast spread for miles around."

"You are saying there is no way your government can prove who Agnes is or how she died and no way to prove that Charles had anything to do with it."

"I took a snippet of hair to run a DNA test to confirm if her identity is registered anywhere. But for now, you are correct. We cannot prove Charles was involved."

"Thank you, Taylor. That's the information I required."

"Director?"

"Yes?"

"We're even now. No more special favors."

"We're even when I say we're even, Taylor. Have a good day." The director hangs up and sighs.

What a shit show. "Agent, call off surveillance on Charles Innocenti. We have nothing on him. Begin researching the bomb evidence used on Ms. Yu's plane in Mexico. Something found on the ground may connect him to wrongdoing."

Chapter 33

Charles - Months Later - Finney House

The Finney family room, decorated in dark rattan furniture with plush cushions, contrasts Blair's Walmart tastes from years ago. Albert chose the stylish and expensive furniture.

The walls say "relax" with an inviting muted blue/grey. They provide an unobtrusive background to Albert's nature scenes that reflect the island's wildlife. A peacefulness envelops me until Buddy tears into the room, diving onto an oversized stuffed elephant a fan had sent.

"Uncle Charles, how did you learn to live in the jungle with lions and tigers and bears?"

"Buddy, no bears live in the African jungles. Those three animals are together in the Wizard of Oz movie only."

"We watch that movie every year on Thanksgiving. But, Uncle Charles, how come you didn't get eaten by a lion or crocodile?" He asks while torturing the elephant's back.

"Jungles exist everywhere, little man. Towns are jungles of people. I learned to be cautious there first."

"Huh?" Buddy falls off the elephant and rolls on the floor with it. I wait until he finishes playing.

"I used a computer first…the information highway.

I studied hard before I even stepped foot on African soil."

"What did you study?"

"I learned where to find water, fruits, and foods to survive. I learned about each animal that kills to eat and how their prey avoids them. You learn those things, and you can understand how to survive."

"That's it?"

"That's it? If you had a lion after you, what would you do?"

"I…I don't know, Uncle."

"Hm. What about a hyena?"

"I don't know that either."

"I see. Would you swim up to a hippopotamus?"

"The ones in the water…those big, fat things? Sure, it wouldn't hurt anyone."

"Wrong. A hippo could chomp me in two in a second. And you—probably, swallow you whole. Hippos kill more people than other predators in Africa, even though they usually eat grass.

"But if you surprise them, they will attack and drown you, flip your boat over, stomp you to death, and I've even seen them eat meat when they are starving. So, stay away from them too."

Buddy's eyes show terror, but not enough that he doesn't want to hear more. "What else would eat me in the jungle?"

"Crocodiles—nasty buggers. Even though they are part of life's cycle, I avoid them."

"Captain Hook doesn't like them either, Uncle Charles. Why don't you like them?"

Hm. The questions aren't going to end anytime soon. I close my computer and invite Buddy to sit on the arm of my recliner.

"Crocs eat baby animals while they are learning to drink from a watering hole. They don't care about what they eat. They grab an animal or a person and take them for a death roll, drowning them. Then they eat. I listened to a mother's cry afterward. So, never jump into a pond in Africa unless you know there are no crocodiles in it."

"What else would swallow me, and how would I get away from them so they couldn't eat me?" Buddy becomes interested in my hair, stroking it like it's a pet. He is built like his father but has his mother's sweet face.

"Unless you are in the Serengeti, lions don't climb trees. So, if you are near lions, make sure there's a tree to climb or, better yet, thorn bushes to hide you. Lions don't like thorns in their paws or anywhere else."

"There's a spaghetti place? Do lions eat spaghetti in trees, Uncle?" Buddy yawns.

"You are one sleepy little man." I swallow a chuckle. "No, lions don't eat spaghetti. They only eat meat. But there is a place in Africa called the Se-ren-get-ti. For some reason, in that place, lions began to climb trees. It isn't natural for them. You won't see them climb trees anywhere else in Africa.

"Since they aren't good at climbing trees, I suggest you climb fast and high if no thorny bushes are nearby. But before you climb a tree, you better check that no leopards are hiding in it. You don't want them to pounce on you."

"Did you ever fight one of those big cats?"

"A lioness once. I have the scar to prove it. See? A claw made it. But other wild cats? No, they don't care for the taste of humans unless they are famished… that means very hungry. But if they believe you are going to hurt them and there is no place for them to run, they will fight and kill you.

"And you'd have to watch out for hyenas—nasty scavengers. A new mom might hunt for food on her own; otherwise, they run in packs. Either way, they don't scare easily. Climb a tree to save yourself. They will wait, but when they realize no food is dropping, Hyenas will move on."

"Do lions eat hynies too, Uncle?"

"Hy-een-ahs. No, lions kill them because they are a nuisance—a pest that steals everyone's food. But lions don't normally eat hyenas; they eat their kill otherwise."

"Did you see elephants and rhinosasauurasuses?"

I almost smile. Am I growing soft? "Yes, I lived with elephants and rhinos, also called Rhi-no-se-ros."

"Did they try to eat you?"

"No, they eat greens, little man—grasses, tree leaves for the most part. But if you bug the bull elephant, he will stomp you flat as a pancake."

"Ha! Like a pancake? Whoa."

"A family of elephants will do everything possible to protect their young. You don't want to get in their way either."

"Or I'll be flat as a pancake?"

"Kersplatt."

"Ha-ha! Kersplatt." The kid mimics me. "Will Rhinos pancake me too, Uncle?"

"First, they'll rush you and gorge you with their big tusk that sits in the middle of their head. You don't want a bony horn going right through you, do you?"

"No, sir. Yuck. That would hurt."

"Yes, it hurts." I think of Carson, who carries the scar of a horn that pierced his leg when he climbed a tree too slowly. "I'll have Carson send you a photo of the scar on his leg. He was lucky the rhino didn't yank him off the tree and stomp on him. You can never be too careful in the jungle."

"Does everything in the jungle want to kill everything else?"

"No, little man. The gazelles aren't carnivorous, which means they don't eat meat. They love the grasses of Africa. They resemble the deer here. They share the grass with water buffalo and giraffes. Unless you bother them first, anything that eats salad greens won't come after you. Then watch out."

My nephew mouths the word carnivorous. He's listening, after all. So, I continue. "In Africa, everything appears different than here. Many animals are beautiful and one of a kind, but some are darn right ugly, like vultures.

"What are vultures, Uncle?"

"The cleanup crews. They are big birds that eat the carcasses of dead animals. That way, diseases don't spread from rotting animals."

Buddy thinks for a few seconds. "How did you know a dangerous animal was close to you?"

I haven't answered so many questions in all my years. "I watch for signs like herds taking off suddenly or birds flushed out of the bush. Sometimes, monkeys stop their noise-making to hide from predators. Again, I learned all I could on a computer and then went on safaris in Africa where guides taught me how to track."

"What's track, Uncle?" Buddy falls onto my lap, barely missing my incision. I let him lay where he lands, hoping he will fall asleep, yet hoping he won't.

"When you look at the ground, you can see the

footprints of animals and other signs. I immediately learned the tracks of predators, including poisonous snakes like the Black Mamba. Their venom, that's the poison in their bite, can kill in a few hours.

"And I read the signs of broken grass, bark off trees, and of course, I knew what every animal's feces and urine looked and smelled like."

"What's feces and urine?"

"Poop and pee, Buddy."

"Poop and pee? Oh, gross, Uncle Charles. You smelled poop?"

"Poop tells you which animal has left it and how long ago it passed out of their body. If you come upon a lion's poop and it smells fresh, would you follow it or stay clear of its path?"

"Oh, no, I'd stay far away from fresh poop because a lion might be close. I see what you mean."

"The same goes for pee clever, boy. You learn quickly."

"I'm glad a lion didn't eat you, Uncle." Buddy gazes up into my eyes adoringly.

"Me too, but I came close to being eaten when I was new to Africa; I was careless. I stopped tracking as I walked, mesmerized by the beautiful sites around me. I didn't pay attention for a few minutes, and when the lion saw me, I couldn't outrun him."

"Did you climb a tree?"

"No trees were close enough. But I slowly backed behind a thick patch of thorn bushes and crawled into the middle. They protected me. See my arms? I still have scars from those bushes, but they saved my life. The lion waited for me to come out of hiding but finally moved on. I learned a lesson that day—never think you are safe in Africa—not for a minute, not for a second."

"I bet lions run fast, too."

"Yes, but not as fast as cheetahs, the fastest wildcat. Cheetahs run up to sixty to seventy miles per hour—that is as fast as a car. There is no outrunning a cheetah in a short sprint. But they can't run fast for long. The best thing is to avoid them. Again, that's where tracking comes in."

"And smelling poop and pee. Ha-ha!"

"What's so funny?" Blair peeks around the corner.

"Me, apparently." Baffled at the emotions inside me, I smile.

Buddy takes my hand and plays with my fingers, "Mommy, Uncle smells poop in Africa." My nephew slides down to the floor with a huge belly laugh.

"Your son wanted to know about my survival in the jungle. He enjoys the tracking story the best, I think."

"Ah, yes, tracking. That does involve knowing whose poop belongs to whom."

"Mommy said poop," Buddy laughs as Blair catches him in a hug.

"All right, Mr. Funnyman, it's time for bed and time for Uncle Charles's meds."

"Aw, Mommy."

"Say goodnight, Buddy."

"Will you tell me more about Africa tomorrow?"

"I will, little man. I'll tell stories about baboons, chimps, and gorillas. Goodnight, Buddy."

"Goodnight, Uncle Charles. Baboons. That's a funny word. Mommy, did you know rhinos have horns right in the middle of their heads like a unicorn?"

"Yes, I do."

"Uncle Charles knows someone who got horned by

one."

"Horned?"

"Can we have pancakes for breakfast because I'll be famished. Ha. Baboon."

As their voices disappear down the hallway, I shake my head—spaghetti-eating lions. I hadn't realized how amusing a child could be and eagerly anticipate another talk with Buddy.

Chapter 34

Recuperating in my sister's home comforts me, strangely. I envision my beloved Africa; I miss it. But the human trafficking programs implemented in America had taken off in the past few weeks, thanks to Debbie, who readied special housing immediately after a rescue.

Her shelters are based on studies of the already established homes for escaped children—smaller programs with little funding and no advertising. But we would need many more homes for the victims. Debbie's system would provide transportation to the homes as soon as The Defenders free trafficked children. Immediately, they would receive counseling and nurturing that includes emotional support animals saved from local shelters.

Meanwhile, personnel investigate the victim's family of origin to understand the child and how their capture originated. Older victims learn skills. Then, they are situated away from high crime areas to begin their new lives with proficiencies.

Traffickers disappear within the first four months of implementing the program elsewhere. Of course, a liver operation and staying with Blair give me a perfect alibi. No one understands my encryptions that bounce around the world to multiple sites before they reach their destinations.

I'm pleased the program has begun to bear positive results, but it must pick up speed to be effective. Soon after arriving in South Africa, I initiated a system to pay female volunteers who protect species and eliminate poachers. They, in turn, recruited other women like them, explaining the benefits. That is how the program took hold like wildfire.

I returned all The Defender's money to the system to promote its growth and continuity. But I'm concerned about using the same program with the same results in America. I had seen all American women as pampered, soft, and squeamish—unable to eradicate vermin like stalkers, predators, and kidnappers.

Persistence found an underlying group of angry, disenfranchised mothers, proving my perspective wrong. Volunteers in secret meetings throughout the States report that these intense women are strong enough to decimate evil. But trainers say they are reckless and not prone to following a regimen as quickly as in Africa, probably because their children aren't starving and already attend a public school system.

Still, Carson sends instructors to carry out each program to the letter. Nothing can be traced back to the Defender, no matter how the law tries. Will independent Americans with full bellies follow procedure? It may be more difficult, but once they reach deep into their pioneering resources, American women might be the most capable yet.

I bet Samantha could find a way to break through my encoding. It's a good thing she was on The Defender's side, funneling money to us through the years. She could have whipped American moms into shape for the program, too. My heart feels a tug. *Don't think about it.*

Still, when her death pops into my brain, I cannot deny the anger that swells within me, along with the damn yank on my heart that makes me question my real nature.

****

Sam's friends schedule a public memorial for her months after they learn of her death. The hospital releases Debbie just in time for it. Greg wheels his wife to an adjacent meeting room in the chapel. Everyone is already there: Blair, Albert, Meghan, Will and me. Sam's death is still unbelievable to everyone. The women sigh in unison.

Before the service begins, they reminisce about Samantha, the first spark that moved me toward my world-renowned status. Only I know that she died upset, heartbroken over my trick to send her back to the States.

As the others chat, I wonder if I even have a heart. I don't remember feeling much or ever loving. My need to eliminate Seth Overmeyer was an attempt to rid myself of my inherent psychopathic tendencies. I had promised Blair I did not kill Seth, and, in truth, I hadn't. I had merely contacted him online so that he would want to meet me—photographing my private parts, making sure he could see a glimpse only before the photo faded off his screen.

Even then, I had skills for remaining untraceable on his computer. Finding an undetectable gun proved less complicated than I thought it would be. I bought it out of state with fake identification and then filed off all markings.

Seth assured me his parents' weekend trip would leave him alone for an entire night. I showed him what turned me on that night. I'd hold a gun to my head and pull the trigger. I told him it made me very horny. I provocatively dressed when I met him at his house. I danced to some loud rock and roll music as I stripped off my top.

Finally, I sat on the overstuffed chair in his bedroom while he lay on the bed, watching as I put the muzzle in my mouth, licked it, and fondled it. I pulled the trigger a couple of times, showing him how aroused it made me.

Seth stayed mesmerized and under my control. I insisted it would make us both so attracted to one another if he did it, too. I told him he could do anything he wanted to me if he would let me watch him hold the gun to his head and pull the trigger. Spreading my legs wide, I reach under my skirt, moaning that he could only touch it if he pulled the trigger.

"Make me want you, Seth."

A pubescent psychopath is still pubescent, after all. He reached for the gun and sat back on his bed.

"Spread your legs more, so I can see, and I'll do it, bitch."

Things could go badly. Seth could turn the gun toward me and pull the trigger. That's why I left one click before the actual bullet. But he doesn't threaten me.

"Do one for practice, Seth. Then I'll take my panties off." He was quick to oblige; I paid him with a full view. I could see his arousal through his pants.

"I told you, Seth. I told you it would make you want me, and I so want you."

"I want to stick it in you. I want to stick it in every hole you have."

"Oh, Seth. Once more. Suck on the gun. Suck it and pull the trigger once more, and you can do whatever you want to me. Oh, Seth." I moaned like I couldn't wait.

I'll never forget that sickening laugh before he pulled the trigger that splattered his brain against the headboard. The rest was clean up, removing any trace of my DNA with a vacuum and wiping down the gun, then pressing his hand and fingers on it.

Masochist magazines placed under his bed full of guns, chains, and whips would lead detectives to realize how disturbed the boy was and that it was enough to commit suicide.

****

I slipped into bed feeling heroic. I had freed the neighborhood of a potential serial killer, and that gratification catapulted me to my purpose.

Eradicating evil-doers may not have destroyed the anomaly within me, but it did twist me enough to use those inclinations in an arena with positive results. Everything had come together except for Sam's death.

Around the world, news shows and television reporters celebrate The Defenders and me. Fans regard Sam's killing as murder but vindicated my organization and me. After all, bad apples turn up everywhere. The Defenders would not pay for Agnes's sins.

But even before the American trafficking program officially begins, some circulars and broadcasters complain about increasing gunfire and bodies dumped in alleyways without due process. They focus on the death of traffickers by rogue vigilantes instead of the children that were saved.

Again, I question whether my plan will work in the USA. Lone vigilantes followed sloppy tactics, but everyone blames The Defenders instead of them. Only time will tell if my program will work without the law clamping down.

To counteract the divisiveness in the media, Albert paints a series on The Defenders. Huge canvases depict me in action. Although shadows always obscure my facial identity, his themes present me as a savior of animals and children. It makes me feel good.

Albert incorporates a hidden peace sign somewhere in the paintings, a symbol of the intended result of my programs. His copyrighted prints sell faster than any other artist on the Internet, and Albert donates fifteen percent to The Defenders.

A knock on the door pulls everyone out of their reveries. It is time for the service to start. We join the crowd in the chapel. The ladies and their husbands file into the front row with me next to them when the music begins.

Mourners from all social classes cram the chapel, flaunting a diversity of sexual persuasions in Sam's honor. Attendees overflow into the hallways and out the doors onto the sidewalk, where speakers broadcast the service.

The flower-filled altar displays photos of Samantha from birth to the present and surrounds the small ebony box filled with trinkets dear to our friend. Individuals stand and regale us with Sam stories. Everyone related to her love of life, people, and saving animals. Most anecdotes are funny, especially about her karaoke experiences, although I have never heard her sing.

I remain silent during the memorial, feeling wholly responsible for her death. In my head, over and over, I repeat my apologies to Sam. I made financial reparations for Sam's elderly parents and the Jose Ramirez family. But nothing could erase the scar from my legacy. More importantly, nothing will bring Samantha back to life. Or back to me. I'm confused by the shadow on my heart when I think of her. What is it?

Perhaps Blair's children mollified me too much. Like little chimps who want nothing more than love and food from their parents, they conjure smiles from their Uncle Charles and bring about a lightheartedness I had never experienced. They seem to be opening my heart or creating one for me. I can't describe it, but I feel peace among the Finney clan.

"Charles, say something before the service is over." Debbie urges me against my will. I glare at her at first but then think better of it. Standing to face the congregation, I wear a low-brimmed fedora and a turned-up collar. I hope it is enough to camouflage my face. We banned photography at the service.

As soon as I stand, the crowd murmurs. "It's him. The Defenders president…" Applause breaks out.

"Please stop. I said stop. This is no time for praise, especially for me. While I appreciate the world's understanding and forgiveness regarding my employee's part in Samantha's demise, this is not about me.

"I've heard memorable anecdotes about Samantha today and realize how much she was loved. She deserves all the love, too.

"I want to share that The Defender's first rehabilitation home for victims of human trafficking has opened. We call it The Samantha Yu House, as will every first home in each country be named. We took our lead from shelters that opened before this cause became known to the general population. We thank them for their suggestions and help.

"Our homes include shelter animals trained in

emotional support known to soothe and re-open damaged hearts as Sam would have wanted."

A sudden heaviness overcomes me, and my breathing becomes shallow. A tear escapes down my cheek, and then more begin to fall. My fingers are wet from wiping away the river flowing down my face.

No, not now.

"I need an emotional support dog, too, today," I say with my hands covering my face. "I miss Sam terribly."

"Do you? Do you really?" A hunched-up figure all in black pushes a walker up the aisle. Each limp forward seems agonizing as the person teeters. "Or are you a skilled actor using a funeral to push your killing machine?"

"What? What are you saying?" I had trouble understanding the stranger, as her words seemed jumbled and unintelligible yet projected like a call in the jungle. Soon, the figure stood before me and removed the veil that had hidden her face, scarred and disfigured, revealing a toothless mouth and misaligned jaws.

"Don't you recognize me, my love?" The voice is altered but still reveals a Chinese accent.

I reach out, touching her brokenness. "Samantha?"

Samantha pushes her walker out of the way and falls into my arms.

"Sam's alive. Sam!" My spontaneity surprises me as emotions roar to the surface. This feeling—this is love. Finally, I feel love. I pull Sam closer, hugging her tightly and stroking her hair. Her appearance stuns everyone.

Then, as the crowd realizes she is alive, their recognition reaches heights of pandemonium and jubilation. Sam reaches into her cloak. My smile turns to shock as I grunt from the searing pain. I can't move as she twists the knife deeper. I deserve it; I know.

I stare into her eyes as the taste of blood rises to my mouth.

"I love you, Sam."

I sink to my knees.

Then, she slices my throat.

Chapter 35

Meghan

I hear voices repeating like a horrible song in a chorus round. "She killed him. Someone killed him."

Shouts escalate to a babbling roar that changes pitch, becoming higher and higher until I cover my ears as I sit like a petrified stone. Am I dreaming? Is this some horror movie? Finally, I search the eyes of my friends. Terror and disbelief flashed on their faces, too. Blair is the first to stand and move robotically toward Charles. She kneels to the body that gurgles, eyes open, life disappearing. Blair screams and rolls her brother over, holding him in her arms as Albert rushes to her side.

I turn my attention to my old friend turned murderer. Sam hobbles around to face the crowd, dropping her black robe. She poses in panties only, showing off jagged, raw scars stitched together along her torso. Bolts stick out of her legs and ribs.

She gazes at the crowd in front of her and speaks. "My fucking parachute didn't open all the way." Sam cackles with an uncontrollable laugh of insanity. "I stay alive for one reason." Her fragmented sentences and her piercing voice quiet the room. Everyone remains in place. "To tell you that Charles Innocenti is a liar, a cad. Look at me." She spreads her arms in a crucifixion pose with hands soaked in blood that runs down her arms.

"This happens when you fall in love with a fucking crazy man. He will never hurt me or anyone else ever again." Samantha guffaws. "Damn parachute."

With a lopsided, grotesque smile, she reaches for the walker and strolls up the aisle, calmly leaving the bloody scene behind. "Yeah, yeah. Take a good look. How you like it, ay? They say I'm a miracle. Is this body a miracle? Aiya."

When Sam reaches the entrance, she breaks into song. "I did it my way." Her screech shocks everyone who stands too close.

Debbie recovers her wits before me. She spins around in her wheelchair, screaming at those in the aisle. "Get out of the way." I'm not far behind as I weave my way through the onlookers.

Deb catches up to Samantha outside on the handicapped walkway. She says nothing but engages at full speed, hitting her from behind. Sam's walker flies forward, causing her to belly-flop onto the curb.

Wheeling to Sam's feet, Debbie screams. "It wasn't him, you fool. Charles didn't kill you! His crazy secretary did, you idiot. Charles loved you! You hear? He loved you."

Now, the runaway walker rolls into the road. A car swerves to miss it, careening onto the sidewalk, plowing through the overflow of mourners. Hats fly into the air. I hear screams as a pink football flies across the walk and lands in a tiny patch of grass.

The out-of-control car knocks Sam's head backward, then rams Debbie's wheelchair up against the pillared portico, where it screeches to a stop. The tragedy happens in a slow-motion nightmare.

Debbie's head is stuck, tilted back. Her body

contorts, her knees pushed to her chin by the automobile's bumper. Her eyes, still open, stare vacantly. The back of her head split open against the column. She is gone.

Sam's remains lay crumpled on the sidewalk with the back tire still sitting on her legs; her neck lay backward, broken.

Quickly, well-meaning guests try to assist the living, ignoring my friends, who are beyond anyone's care.

Although I know nothing of first aid or triage, I meander through the carnage aimlessly. I wonder how Charles would feel now. Is killing outside the law still worth it, Charles?

My eyes fall upon a pink lump on the ground—a baby weeks old. It must have been the football I saw flying out of the arms of a loving parent who is dead or maimed somewhere around me.

Carefully, I support her back and neck as I cradle the limp baby to my chest. "Please let her be alive. Please." She utters a gurgle, a movement, and then a wail. "She's alive. She's alive." I scream to the heavens ecstatically. Joy, love, and hope fill me all at once.

Approaching sirens blare, drowning me out yet assuring me that help has arrived. My emotions fly high while I gingerly cradle the crying infant as if she were the last baby on Earth. I haven't felt anything this intense since the birth of my babies.

Yet, this wonder reveals itself uniquely when saving a life. Wait. Is this what Charles feels with each animal he saves? Each poacher he kills? Am I experiencing his purpose? That he wanted only to save lives?

I pass the infant to an EMT, who is all business as I explain her flight and fall. I'm feeling overprotective, like a new mother with her first baby, as he places her on a gurney, examining every inch.

"Ma'am, please go on now; we need room to move. We'll take good care of her."

Reluctantly, I back away to find William when I spot three adults in a pile, like dominoes fallen over, as though each tried to protect the other from the oncoming vehicle. The man on top of the heap is breathing, and the teenager on the bottom moans. It must be the mother in the middle with the gash on her head. I call out again.

"These people are still alive but hurt badly!"

One emergency technician comes running, and I wish I could help. But I don't have the medical knowledge to do more. An understanding envelops me as my rigid brain shatters like glass. My heart softens to my new truth when William reaches out.

"Thank God, Meghan, you are okay. Are you hurt at all?"

"Oh, Will, I won't ever judge another person."

"Megs, what are you talking about?"

"Charles…maybe he loved life, saving lives, more than killing them. Odd, as Samantha always believed in him while I didn't. Now, she slaughters him, and I can only defend him. She was wrong. I was wrong. Oh, Will."

"God, she's dead. My Debbie, my Debbie is dead." I hear Greg's voice above the fray.

Blair and Albert rush to his side; everyone weeps over a wasted miracle. I drop down to a step, too shaken to stand as the shock takes its course. William sits by me, doing his best to ignore the carnage.

"Will… one moment in time and look what happens. If Sam had died in the plane, Debbie and Charles would be alive. We'd be ordering lunch and reminiscing. Did you see her? Our vibrant Sam turned into an insane monster. She survived a bombing, but she held Charles responsible for her condition. She didn't know about his employee being the guilty party—or didn't believe it.

"Her hatred must have given her strength to go on, to plan Charles's murder, which brought about this entire atrocity. Sam didn't know she changed Charles for the better. I don't think she heard his 'I love you, Sam.' I bet he never said those words to any other living soul. He finally feels love, but it murders him."

Will wraps both arms around me, and I lean into him as screams and shouts echo. "What do we do now?"

"We support Blair, your one remaining friend. I'll help Greg as best as I can. But you know that Debbie was his life. It's going to be rough."

"No, William. I mean, what do we do now about The Defenders? Can it continue without Charles?"

"Meghan, you see the result of violence? No one dies without a loved one somewhere grieving the loss, too, and the repercussions go on—like this scene. That's why I'm against using force of any kind."

Will stares at the ground, unable to deal with the bloodbath around him. He attended this funeral only to support me. Usually, he avoids death or anything to do with it.

But I can't take my eyes off the devastation as more rescue vehicles and police arrive. It seems like a documentary that I'm talking over. "Odd. I used the law as a weapon against Charles. But in time, I had come to admire his results. Look at what The Defenders accomplished. Their actions fast-tracked protection for all animals. What could it have done for trafficked children?"

"Don't count The Defenders out. Charles was brilliant. He said the plan was already in place, although I disagree with his methods. Time will tell."

I ignore my husband's attempt to console me and continue with a new attitude and resolve. "Plugging along in the legal system, drafting laws doesn't seem much to me now. Just because I won't use a gun doesn't mean I can't support those who do."

"That's a 360-degree turnaround for you. You don't plan to carry on for Debbie and Charles, do you? You must be in shock. You don't believe in violence."

"Will, I don't believe in vengeance as Sam did. But now, witnessing all this bloodshed and finding a baby alive against all the odds, I've experienced how precious each innocent life is. Maybe Charles understood that years ago. I empathize with his war now because victims don't have time on their side. Charles refused to wait for obtuse lawmakers and their excessive red tape required to pass laws. So, he fixed the problem by killing evil monsters to save the innocent.

"Yes, I want to be a part of The Defenders."

"No. You are suffering from shock, I'm telling you. Come on, let's help Blair, Albert, and most of all, Greg."

My mood drops a little, knowing my husband fears involvement in any vigilante system as he escorts me to the crowd surrounding Debbie. When I view my friend's lifeless form, now in Greg's lap, rocked back and forth as a father might coddle a toddler, my body shakes, and my heart breaks. He strokes Debbie's hair, spreading the blood. No one stops him.

Will takes one glimpse and vomits. I'm reminded of Debbie's words:

"Ostriches fill the world, hiding their heads in the sand, hoping to avoid unnerving events because if they do see the world as it is, a change would be required. Most wouldn't know how to effect a change, let alone become the change."

Charles was the rare one, going after trouble, becoming the difference. He changed the world, finding happiness in the process. Charles lit up with unmistakable love and joy when he saw Samantha, as broken as she was.

As though she reads my mind, Blair, blood-soaked from hugging Charles, reaches out her hand. Without hesitation, I grasp it; we fall into one another's arms. We hug fiercely, locked together.

"Please, Blair, tell me it isn't too late to support The Defenders. Charles was right all along. I was wrong. I'm sorry it's taken so long for me to see it. I'm so ashamed of myself. Promise me that we won't let them die in vain. Please, promise me."

"Oh, Meghan, we've both endured a long road of twists and turns to arrive at this point. I didn't believe in his cause completely, but now I do. I don't think Charles was evil, but even if he was, he twisted it, only using it for good. Maybe he believed sincerely in justice and loved too hard even though he couldn't define it as love.

"I promise for Charles, Debbie, and Sam, our old Sam, The Defenders will live on."

"No matter what, Blair?"

"No matter what, Megs."

A word about the author...

Seven Rodgers discovered a passion for writing fiction in 2010. Since then, she has written five novels and finds writing a natural extension to her eighteen-year career as an entertainer, writing award-winning music and lyrics.

Rodgers attended the University of North Florida, Jacksonville. For thirty-five years, she lived on Amelia Island, in Florida. She moved to St. Croix in the Virgin Islands where she snorkeled for pleasure, wrestled a fixer upper into submission, and wrote Dream of Me.

She recently moved to the Smokey's in Franklin, North Carolina.

Seven has one grown son, Luke, and three stray dogs that adopted her.

www.7rodgers.com

www.ingramcontent.com/pod-product-compliance
Lightning Source LLC
Chambersburg PA
CBHW052024020726
47501CB00004B/1238